LOST
LAUGHTER

Recent Books by Barbara Cartland

Love, Lords, and Lady-Birds
The Ghost Who Fell in Love
The Chieftan Without a Heart
Flowers for the God of Love
Journey to Paradise
Love in the Clouds
Imperial Splendour
Bride to the King
Dawn of Love
Love for Sale

The Prince and the Pekingese
The Duchess Disappeared
A Nightingale Sang
Terror in the Sun
A Gentleman in Love
The Power and the Prince
Little White Doves of Love
Free from Fear

Barbara Cartland

LOST
LAUGHTER

E. P. Dutton New York

For information contact:
Elsevier-Dutton Publishing Co., Inc., 2 Park Avenue,
New York, N.Y. 10016

Library of Congress Cataloging in Publication Data

Cartland, Barbara.
Lost laughter.

I. Title.
PZ3.C247Lks   1980   [PR6005.A765]   823'.912
80-12897

ISBN: 0-525-14891-4

Published simultaneously in Canada by
Clarke, Irwin & Company Limited, Toronto and Vancouver

10 9 8 7 6 5 4 3 2 1
First   Edition

Author's Note

The Fleet Prison, which stood near the Fleet Market in London, was where debtors were taken and forced to stay until they were either bailed out or their debts were paid by their friends and relatives.

Tobias Smollett, who was imprisoned for libel, wrote a book which explained how the prisoners were treated.

Everything depended, as in other prisons, on having money with which to bribe the jailors and to be able to purchase what they required from the innumerable hawkers, tradesmen, and shops in the vicinity.

There was, however, a worse hazard in the prisons even than being without money.

This was the "gaol fever" which swept through all the prisons at this time due to insanitary conditions and bad water. Being taken to the Fleet meant that one lost not only one's freedom but very often one's life.

This is the first novel I have written in which the hero has been a Viscount. This title dates from the beginning of the Tenth Century and is descended from the Office of Deputy or Lieutenant (Vice-Comes) of a Count.

Henry VI, Crowned King of England and France, created John Lord Beaumont in 1440 Viscount Beaumont in England and Vicomte Beaumont in France.

The title received precedence above all Barons, but it did not become popular until the Seventeenth Century.

The eldest son of a Marquis or an Earl is often give the honorary title of Viscount, but in this case he is not allowed to sit in the House of Lords.

Chapter One
1818

The Viscount Ockley tore out of the house, took the steps with a leap, and threw himself into his Phaeton.

He picked up the reins and brought the whip down on the backs of his horses, which made them spring forward so violently that the stable-boy who had been holding their heads only just had time to jump clear.

Then the Phaeton was away, swaying as the horses galloped at an unprecedented speed down the drive, the gravel flying out behind, and the Viscount took the turn at the lodge-gates on one wheel.

The dust from the narrow country road was billowing out behind and the villagers stared in astonishment as he sped past them.

He had driven for nearly three miles before the horses slowed down a little. He appeared not to notice, but sat staring ahead, his eyes dark with anger, his lips in a tight line.

He was an exceedingly good-looking man, with

clear-cut features, a determined chin, and a breadth of shoulder which made him an outstanding pugilist in Gentleman Jackson's Boxing Academy.

He was also considered a Corinthian when he had the right horses to drive, and he was a formidable contestant in any Steeple-Chase.

It was inevitable that he should be a social success with the Fair Sex, especially as he moved amongst the Bucks and Beaux who had nothing better to do, when they were not losing a fortune at cards, than to discuss the latest "Incomparables."

There was no doubt that Miss Niobe Barrington had taken the vacillating hearts of these gentlemen by storm, which was not surprising considering that she was not only beautiful but a considerable heiress.

Her father, Sir Aylmer Barrington, was not just "warm in the pocket," as the current slang put it. He was a very rich man indeed, and he made sure that everybody was aware of it.

He intended that his only daughter should command attention and he made sure of it by giving a Ball that for sheer expenditure exceeded any other that was likely to take place during the Season.

He was also prepared to offer his hospitality to every aristocrat who was willing to accept it, the proviso being that they were eligible bachelors and participants in the matrimonial stakes for Niobe's hand in marriage.

The Viscount, who was noted as having a roving eye which never missed an attractive woman, was completely bowled over the first time he saw Niobe.

He had accepted reluctantly the impressive, somewhat pretentious card of invitation he found waiting for him at White's Club, simply because he had nothing else to do that evening.

He also found that most of his contemporaries had likewise decided to put in an appearance at Sir Aylmer's house in Grosvenor Square, though they had gone prepared to be sceptical, having in the past found that heiresses on the whole had nothing to recommend them except a large Bank-balance.

That Niobe was different was an understatement.

She was ravishingly beautiful, with hair the colour of ripening corn, eyes of periwinkle blue, and the type of skin which had sent poets into a frenzy of creation since the beginning of time.

When her blue eyes looked up into the Viscount's grey ones, he was lost.

From that moment he had pursued Niobe with an ardour that had surprised even his closest friends.

This not only surprised but delighted his creditors, who had almost despaired of ever having their accounts, which grew longer and longer every year, settled.

His tailor had actually opened a bottle of wine at home with his wife when he heard that the Viscount was likely to be "leg-shackled" to one of the richest heiresses to appear on the social horizon since the war.

"I would not care if she had not a penny to her name!" the Viscount told his closest friend, the Honourable Frederick Hinlip.

"She would care if she had to live in that ramshackle mansion of yours without having the means to do it up," Freddy replied, "and you know as well as I do that you need some new horses."

The Viscount had the grace to look somewhat shame-faced.

"You know I am grateful for the loan of yours, Freddy."

"You are welcome," his friend replied with a grin, "except that I would sometimes like to ride them myself!"

"She is the most beautiful thing I have ever seen!" the Viscount exclaimed raptly, forgetting for the moment the usually absorbing subject of horse-flesh.

"I agree with you, but do not forget that you marry not only her but her father."

"What do you mean by that?"

"Sir Aylmer is as hard as nails and as tough as a rhinoceros. He is looking for the best for his Niobe, and who shall blame him?"

"Are you insinuating that I am not good enough for her?" the Viscount asked.

"I have heard that Porthcawl is being unusually attentive."

"That old nit-wit!" the Viscount scoffed. "He has a flabby hand-shake and always reminds me of a wet codfish!"

"He is also a Marquis!"

"The idea of Niobe even looking in his direction is laughable," the Viscount said loftily.

However, he had felt slightly apprehensive as to what was happening when Niobe had told him a week ago that her father did not favour him as a suitor.

"What do you mean by that?"

"Exactly what I say," Niobe had replied. "Papa thinks you are too irresponsible to make me a good husband. In fact, dear Valient, I fear that he is going to forbid you the house."

"Then we must run away—elope!" the Viscount said firmly.

Niobe looked at him wide-eyed, and he said:

"I will get a Special Licence so there will be no need to go posting off to Gretna Green or any of that nonsense. We will be married at the first Church we come to. Once you are my wife, there will be nothing your father can do about it."

"He will be very angry," Niobe said. "Besides, I would like a grand wedding with bridesmaids and a huge Reception afterwards."

"That is exactly what you shall have, my darling, if your father will give his consent to our marriage," the Viscount urged. "But if he refuses, there will be nothing we can do except take matters into our own hands."

Niobe had risen from the sofa on which they were sitting to walk with what she knew was exquisite grace across the room to the window.

The house in Park Lane had a garden behind it and she was well aware that, silhouetted against the green of the trees, with the sunshine on her golden head, she was a picture of allurement.

The Viscount watched her as if he was bewitched.

"You are so beautiful—so exquisitely beautiful!" he cried. "How could I lose you?"

She gave him a beguiling little smile and in a moment he was on his feet and had taken her in his arms.

"I love you! I love you, Niobe!"

Then he was kissing her wildly, passionately, demandingly, and as he felt her respond he knew that there was no need for him to worry about the future.

When they were both breathless, Niobe moved from his arms to say:

"I forgot to tell you that we are going to the country this weekend. Papa has arranged to give another Ball for me for our neighbours who live in Surrey. It will be very exciting, with fireworks, gondolas on the lake, and a Gypsy Orchestra in the garden, besides another in the Ball-Room."

"I am bored with Balls!" the Viscount said petulantly. "I want you to myself. Shall I speak to your father and insist we get married before the end of the Season?"

Niobe held up her hands in horror.

"No, no! It would only incense him and make him definitely refuse to let me see you again."

She paused before she added:

"As it is, you will not be invited to the Ball."

"Do you mean to say that your father disapproves of me to that extent?" the Viscount asked incredulously.

He had never in the whole of his life been barred from any house at which he wished to be a guest, and he found it incredible that Sir Aylmer would dare to ostracise him in this extraordinary fashion.

Niobe cast down her eyes.

"The trouble is, dear Valient, that Papa thinks I am growing too fond of you."

The Viscount's eyes lit up.

"That is what I want you to be, but I want you to say you love me."

"I think I do, I am almost sure of it," Niobe answered, "but Papa says love is one thing and marriage another."

"What does he mean by that?" the Viscount asked angrily.

Niobe gave a little sigh.

"Papa wants me to make a very grand marriage."

The Viscount stared at her as if he was stunned.

"Are you saying," he asked at length, in a voice that sounded strangled in his throat, "that your father does not think I am grand enough socially? I would have you know that the Ockleys consider themselves the equals of any family in the land. There is not a history-book that does not mention us!"

"Yes, yes, I know that," Niobe said quickly. "It is just that Papa has other ideas."

"What ideas?" the Viscount asked ominously.

Niobe made a little gesture with her hands that was very expressive.

"Are you telling me there is someone he favours more than me?" the Viscount asked.

Niobe did not reply and he pulled her back into his arms.

"You are mine and you love me—you know you love me! You must be brave, my darling, and tell your father so."

"He would not listen."

"Then we will run away."

The Viscount was just about to explain how this could be done, when Niobe lifted her lovely face to his and said:

"Kiss me, Valient! I adore your kisses, and I am so afraid of losing you."

The Viscount kissed her until he forgot everything but the allurement of her.

Only when he was driving away from Park Lane did he remember that he had not had time to expound the plans he had begun to make for their elopement.

He had, however, written her a passionate letter which had been conveyed by his valet to Niobe's lady's-maid so that there was no danger of its being intercepted by Sir Aylmer.

In reply he had had two scribbled lines from Niobe telling him to call on her at her father's house in Surrey the following Monday.

The Viscount knew that the Ball to which he had not been invited was to take place on Saturday, and he decided that Niobe wanted to see him alone after the house-party had left.

However, it was infuriating to find that the majority of his friends were staying either at Sir Aylmer's huge mansion or with people in the neighbourhood.

Having nothing else to do, he had driven to Hertfordshire to his own house, knowing he would find it depressing, except that it could easily be restored to its former beauty when Niobe's fortune could be expended on it.

The war had almost bankrupted the Viscount's father, who had not only invested a great deal of money on the Continent but had also had no idea that he should economise personally.

When he died six months after his son had returned to England after fighting with Wellington's Army and spending another year with the Army of Occupation, the new Viscount found he had inherited a house falling to bits through lack of repair, a mountain of debts, and nothing in the Bank with which to settle them.

Because after the long years of war he wished to enjoy himself and make up for what he felt was the loss of his youth, the Viscount had shelved the pressing financial problems which faced him and thrown himself whole-heartedly into the gaieties which were to be found in London.

Regardless of the expense, he had opened up Ockley House in Berkeley Square, shrugged his shoulders at the fact that it was mortgaged to the hilt, and proceeded to live like a Lord, despite the fact, as he had said to Freddy, that he had "holes in his pockets."

It struck him after nearly two years of indulgence that sooner or later he would have to do something about his financial position, and it was obvious that only marriage to an heiress could in fact save him.

This would be no new departure in the Ockley family.

In most generations there had been an Ockley who had followed the dictates of his head rather than his heart and had taken a wife who had brought him either money or land.

And that had been their only asset, the Viscount often reflected cynically as he looked at their portraits hanging on the walls in the family house and thought them an extremely plain if not ugly collection of women.

When he had been camping out on some mountainside in Portugal or fighting in the heat and dust of France, he had found himself thinking romantically of the type of woman he would marry.

He would not have been human if he had not been conscious of his own good looks and the fact that female hearts undoubtedly fluttered in their breasts when he appeared.

He wanted a wife who would be a complement to himself, and he hoped that together they would produce children who would ensure that any future family portraits were an improvement on those of the past.

Niobe had seemed the answer to the soldier's prayer, and from his long experience of women the Viscount was aware that his kisses excited her and there was a gleam in her eyes when she looked at him, which he expected.

When he had driven down to Surrey on Monday morning he had not hurried his horses, despite his impatience to reach Niobe, because they belonged to Freddy.

He told himself that the correct time to call would be in the afternoon.

He had spent the whole of the weekend perfecting his plans for their elopement and was very conscious that in the inside pocket of his close-fitting, well-cut but unpaid-for driving-coat he carried a Special Licence.

"Sir Aylmer may be annoyed," the Viscount ruminated, "but once we are married there will be nothing he can do, and as Niobe has her own money he cannot cut her off with the proverbial shilling."

It certainly had seemed as if everything was as he wished it to be, and yet there was a small nagging doubt in his mind because Niobe had been so insistent on a grand wedding.

It was not in fact the first time she had mentioned it.

He recalled her saying that the Prince Regent had attended the marriage of one of her friends and she would feel chagrined if he was not the guest of honour at hers.

The Viscount had of course met the Regent on various occasions but had felt no particular wish for a closer acquaintanceship, finding that the long-drawn-out dinners at Carlton House were boring and the musical evenings which usually followed made him yawn.

What he enjoyed was frequenting the Gaming-Rooms, the Houses of Pleasure, and the Dance-Halls with his friends who often attended such places merely as spectators or to have what might be described as a "rowdy evening," which unfortunately invariably cost money.

At the same time, they were amusing, as were the night Steeple-Chases, the racing at Newmarket or Epsom, and the hard-drinking dinner-parties which always followed a day on the Turf.

"I am sure His Royal Highness will be delighted to be present at our wedding," the Viscount had said quickly, because it was expected of him.

He knew as he spoke that it was extremely doubtful that the Prince Regent would be there, and if Niobe was disappointed there would be different pleasures he could offer her.

As he drove down the well-kept drive and saw Sir Aylmer's enormous mansion in the distance, the Viscount forgot everything but his desire to be with Niobe.

She was waiting for him in the Salon, which if he had noticed it he would have thought over-luxurious to the point of bad taste.

But he had eyes only for Niobe herself, who rose from a seat by the window as he entered, looking, he thought, even more lovely than when he had last seen her.

Her gown matched the colour of her eyes and revealed the exquisite shape of her body, and while a critic might have thought she was wearing too much jewellery for a young girl in the country, the Viscount saw only the curve of her lips.

He put his arms round her.

"No, Valient! No!" Niobe said, keeping him at arm's length with her long white fingers.

"What do you mean—'no'?" the Viscount enquired.

"You are not to kiss me until you have heard what I have to tell you."

"I have a lot to tell you too."

"You must listen to me first."

Because he wished to please her he forced himself to concentrate on what she was trying to say.

"I am afraid this will upset you, Valient, but Papa agreed that I should tell you myself."

"Tell me what?" the Viscount enquired.

He had dropped his arms, at Niobe's insistence, but now he stood very tall and elegant beside her and found it hard to think of anything but her beauty and the softness of her lips, which he wanted to kiss.

"What I have to tell you," Niobe said, "is that I

have promised to marry the Marquis of Porthcawl!"

For a moment the Viscount found it hard to understand what she was saying. It was almost as if she were speaking a foreign language.

Then as the words penetrated his mind he felt as if someone had struck him a heavy blow on the head.

"Is this some joke?" he asked.

"No, of course not," Niobe replied. "Papa is delighted. We are to be married next month."

"I do not believe it!" the Viscount exclaimed. "If this is your father's plan, then we must do what we have already intended and run away."

Even as he spoke, he knew from the expression on Niobe's face that she would not go with him, but still he had to hear her say so.

"I have a Special Licence," he went on. "We will be married, then it will be impossible for your father to take you from me."

"I am sorry, Valient, I knew this would upset you. Although I love you and I would like to have been your wife, I cannot refuse the Marquis."

The Viscount drew in his breath.

"What you are saying," he said slowly, and his voice was bitter, "is that you have been playing me along just in case Porthcawl did not come up to scratch, but now that he has, you are prepared to drop me like a hot brick!"

He knew as he spoke that this was the truth.

"I am sorry, Valient," Niobe said again, "but I hope that after I am married we can be friends."

It was then that the Viscount lost his temper.

He had always had one. It was something he had inherited from a long line of Ockleys, a temper which was seldom aroused, but when it was it exploded like the charge of a cannon.

Afterwards the Viscount could not remember exactly what he had said to Niobe. He was only aware that as he spoke, not shouting but speaking with a bitter intensity words which cut like a whip, she went very pale.

When she did not reply and he felt there was nothing more to say, he had stormed from the room, intent on putting the greatest distance possible between himself and the woman who had betrayed him.

Now that he found it a little easier to breathe and the constriction in his chest was not so violent, he was aware that his horses, because of the speed at which he had driven them, were sweating and he himself felt unpleasantly hot.

The idea of heat drew his mind to something strange. He looked down on the floor of the Phaeton and saw to his surprise that a rug was lying there in an unusual position.

Then as he looked at it, wondering why he should have brought a rug with him on such a hot day, it moved and he stared in sheer astonishment as a face appeared from under it.

It was a small oval face in which were two dark eyes looking at him a little apprehensively.

"May I come . . . out now?" a small voice asked. "I am very hot."

"Who are you?" the Viscount asked sharply. "And what the devil are you doing here?"

In answer, the rug was thrown to one side and a girl who appeared very slight and small climbed onto the seat beside him.

She was wearing a somewhat crumpled gown and her dark head was bare except that hanging down her back, tied to her neck by two ribbons, was a somewhat unfashionable bonnet.

The Viscount looked at her in astonishment, then back at his horses, and at her again, before he asked:

"I suppose you have some reason for being in my Phaeton?"

"I am running away."

"From whom?"

"From my Uncle Aylmer."

"Are you telling me that Sir Aylmer Barrington is your uncle?" the Viscount asked in a tone of fury.

"Yes."

"Then in that case you can get out! I have no wish to have anything further to do with the Barringtons for the rest of my life!"

"I knew you would feel like that."

"You knew?" the Viscount snapped. "What have you to do with the diabolical manner in which I have been treated?"

"Nothing," came the reply, "except that I watched you being dangled on a string just in case the Marquis got off the hook at the last moment."

The fact that this was what he himself had thought made the Viscount so angry that he pulled his horses to a standstill.

"Get out!" he stormed. "Get out and be damned to you! And you can tell both your uncle and his daughter that I hope they rot in hell!"

The way he spoke and the anger on his face should have intimidated the girl sitting beside him.

Instead, she looked at him with commiseration before she said:

"I am sorry, but actually, although you will not believe me, you have had a very lucky escape."

"What the hell do you mean by that?" the Viscount enquired.

"You do not know Niobe as I do. She is spiteful and unkind and would have made you extremely unhappy."

"I do not believe that Niobe is any of those things, and if you speak like that I shall slap you!" the Viscount threatened.

"That would be nothing new," the girl answered. "When Uncle Aylmer beat me this morning I decided I must run away. That is why I am here."

"Beat you?" the Viscount echoed. "I do not believe you!"

"I will show you the marks if you like," the girl answered. "He is always beating me. When I first came to live with them he did it because Niobe told him to, and after that he enjoyed it!"

The Viscount stared at her in sheer astonishment.

He did not want to believe what he was hearing, but at the same time there was an unmistakable ring of truth in the way the girl spoke that was more convincing than if she had cried or expostulated at his disbelief.

He turned sideways to look at her.

She seemed very young, little more than a child.

"How old are you?" he asked.

"I am eighteen."

"And what is your name?"

"Jemima Barrington."

"And you really are Niobe's cousin?"

"My mother was Sir Aylmer's sister. She ran away from home with my father, who was a distant cousin, and they were very poor but very happy! When they died and I was orphaned, Uncle Aylmer took me to live with him. That is why I know that you have had a lucky escape."

As the conversation returned to him, the Viscount was scowling again.

"I am sorry for you, but you know as well as I do that I cannot involve myself with your troubles. I will take you wherever you want to go, as long as nobody hears about it."

"I do not suppose anybody would be interested," Jemima said. "Niobe dislikes me and Uncle Aylmer finds me an encumbrance."

She gave a little sigh before she said:

"Who worries about a poor relation anyway?"

"Is that what you are?"

"My mother preferred love to riches. She was the exception to the rest of the family."

The Viscount thought that was true.

Niobe had certainly preferred a more important title than the one he himself possessed.

As if she knew what he was thinking, Jemima said:

"Niobe is a snob like her father. She wants to sit with the Peeresses at the Opening of Parliament, and if a Duke appeared at this moment, the Marquis himself would be ditched just as you have been!"

"I told you not to talk like that!" the Viscount warned.

"One day you will know that I am right."

The Viscount was about to retort, then thought it was undignified.

"Where do you want to go?" he asked instead, picking up his reins.

"Anywhere you are prepared to take me."

"Have you any money?"

"Only two guineas, which I stole off Uncle Aylmer's dressing-table."

The Viscount let the reins go slack.

"Are you telling me quite seriously that you are going out into the world on your own with nothing to keep you from starvation except for two guineas?"

There was silence, then Jemima said in a different tone from what she had used before:

"There is nothing else I can do. I cannot go on being beaten, pinched, and slapped, and made so desperately . . . miserably . . . unhappy."

There was a sob in the last words that was very moving, and the Viscount said:

"Have you no other relatives to whom I could take you?"

"They would be too frightened of Uncle Aylmer to do anything but send me straight back to him."

"That is something I should do anyway."

There was a frown on his forehead at the thought of returning, but he told himself that there was nothing else he could do.

Because the thought of going back towards Niobe made his temper flare again, he said angrily:

"Blast you for interfering! All I want is to get away and show that scheming, title-loving cousin of yours what I think of her!"

He laughed scornfully.

"I told her what I would do, and I meant it!"

"What did you tell her?" Jemima asked curiously.

The Viscount's eyes narrowed.

"I told her I would marry the first woman I met rather than let anyone know that she had humiliated me."

The words seemed almost to be spat from his lips. Then he glared ahead, as if he was seeing not the open countryside but Niobe's face growing pale while he raged at her, with at the same time an expression of determination in her blue eyes which told the Viscount that she intended to marry the Marquis.

He wished now he had shaken or half-throttled her, which would have taught her a lesson that men could be as ruthless as women, if nothing else.

Then a soft voice beside him said hesitantly:

"If ... that is what you ... said ... I am the ... first woman you have ... seen."

The Viscount turned his head to look at her.

"My God—so you are!" he said. "And perhaps it would indeed be more appropriate if I married a Barrington."

The words came almost inaudibly from between the tightness of his lips, and he did not look at Jemima but he heard her say:

"Nothing could make ... Niobe more angry ... than that I should be ... married before her—and to you!"

The Viscount gave a little laugh and it was not a pleasant sound.

"There ought to be a Church not far from here."

He whipped up his horses and drove on, thinking as he did so that such a revenge on the woman who had humiliated him would be exceedingly effective.

Because for some years he had been an avowed bachelor, the fact of his marriage, he knew, would cause something of a sensation in the Clubs of St. James's.

That he had been wooing Niobe Barrington ardently and flamboyantly for the last month meant there were undoubtedly bets in the Betting-Box at White's on his success or failure, and it would bring an undoubted touch of irony when it was announced that he had married her cousin.

The Viscount knew Niobe well enough to realise that she always liked to be the centre of the picture, the leading-lady in the drama of her own life.

Some critical part of his mind was aware that she had dramatised every moment of his courtship so that the final denouement, when her marriage was announced, would be, she hoped, the sensation of the Season.

Although she had now caught her Marquis, some of the glitter and the glamour would be gone from it if he had been married first.

There was almost a cruel smile on the Viscount's lips as he drew his horses to a standstill outside the lych-gate which stood at the entrance to a small, grey-stone Church.

"This will do," he said.

He looked round for someone to hold his horses and was beckoning some boys who were looking at the Phaeton in admiration when he heard a small voice say:

"You really mean you will . . . marry me?"

"I presume that is a better situation in which to find yourself than walking the streets of London?"

"Yes . . . yes . . . of course . . . and I am very . . . grateful."

"There is no reason for you to be so," the Viscount replied. "I am doing this to teach your cousin a lesson, and I hope she finds it a painful one."

"She will!" Jemima said.

The Viscount stepped from the Phaeton, having instructed a small boy to hold his horses, and asked where the Vicar was likely to be found.

" 'E be in t' Church, Sir, doin' a Chris'nin'."

The Viscount walked on through the lych-gate, making no effort to assist Jemima down from the Phaeton.

Having managed it herself, she followed him, pulling her bonnet over her untidy hair and tying the ribbons under her chin.

When she reached the porch she stood aside to let a man and a woman, carrying a baby in her arms, followed by several other people, pass her.

When they had done so, she saw the Viscount talking to an elderly man in a surplice.

She smoothed down her creased gown nervously, aware that the Viscount was handing the Vicar a piece of paper.

Then as he walked towards the altar the Viscount beckoned her and she went to stand at his side.

"I have explained that your first name was inadvertently omitted from the Special Licence," he said in a voice that was completely impersonal but with still an undercurrent of anger in it, "and you will answer to Jemima Niobe."

Jemima nodded but seemed for the moment to have lost her voice, and her eyes were very large in her pale face.

The Viscount did not look at her but merely walked up the aisle without offering her his arm, and because she saw that the Vicar was waiting Jemima walked quickly along beside him.

The prayers were short and there was an uncomfortable pause when the Viscount realised he had no ring.

He drew a gold signet-ring from the little finger of his left hand, and because it was too large Jemima had to hold it in place with her finger bent.

The Vicar pronounced them man and wife, the Viscount paid the fee, which was five shillings, and as the Cleric began to offer his congratulations, the Viscount walked away and there was nothing Jemima could do but follow him.

"Thank you . . . thank you very much," she said, realising that the Vicar was looking after the Viscount in surprise at his bad manners.

Then, afraid she might be left behind, Jemima ran down the aisle to catch up with her husband just as he reached the lych-gate.

Chapter Two

Jemima awoke and thought with a little start that she had overslept, then as she opened her eyes she saw a strange bedroom and remembered where she was.

She was also aware that the reason why she had awakened was that somebody had come into the room, and now she saw that it was a maid who was pulling back the curtains.

"What time is it?" Jemima asked.

"After nine o'clock, M'Lady."

Jemima held her breath. The way she had been addressed told her that everything that she thought had happened yesterday was true, although it still seemed like a dream.

When they arrived back in London the horses were tired and so was Jemima, but she had not said so because she was not used to talking about herself or expecting anybody to be interested in what she had to say.

They had driven in silence ever since leaving the

23

Church, the scowl still on the Viscount's face, and when they had reached Berkeley Square and a groom had appeared to take the horses, he had walked ahead in through the front door, leaving Jemima to follow him.

Without saying anything to the waiting servants, he went into a room which Jemima saw was the Library and seated himself at a large desk.

She stood uncomfortably in the doorway, watching him as he drew a piece of crested paper from a leather box and set it in front of him on the blotter.

Then as he picked up a quill-pen Jemima asked:

"What . . . do you want me to do?"

"Wait a minute!" the Viscount replied irritably. "I have to get this announcement off to the *Gazette* so that it will be in the paper tomorrow morning."

"Yes . . . of course," Jemima agreed.

Because there seemed to be no point in standing, she walked farther into the room to sit down in an arm-chair.

Looking round her, she realised that the room, while luxuriously furnished, was somewhat shabby and the tables and china needed dusting.

Then she told herself she must not criticise but should be grateful for the strange fate that had resulted in her having at least a roof over her head and somewhere to sleep tonight.

Everything had happened so quickly that she felt as if she had not had time to consider or even barely to be aware of what she was doing when she married the Viscount.

The only thing that had mattered was that she should not have to go back to be beaten once again by her uncle for running away.

She hated him to the point where even to think of his determined face made her shudder. The beating he had given her this morning had only been one of many that she knew had not only hurt her body but had humiliated her pride and her self-respect.

Never had she imagined it possible that there could be people in the world as cruel, selfish, and unfeeling as Sir Aylmer and his daughter.

She knew that Niobe disliked her because, small and insignificant though she was, she was still a woman and therefore constituted a rival in her cousin's mind.

She had forced her father into beating her in the first place because she was afraid that he might develop a fondness for her, and that in Niobe's mind might detract in some way from his affection for her.

Niobe was possessive, Jemima often thought, to the point where the world must revolve round her and her alone.

If Jemima looked in the least attractive, Niobe took it out on her with pinchings and slaps and, if she denied it, another beating from her father.

At the same time, she made thorough use of Jemima. She had become an unpaid lady's-maid, or rather the word should have been "slave," to her cousin, and sometimes when she had run up and down the stairs a hundred times a day and been told all the time how stupid and ungrateful she was, she would be so tired and miserable at night that she was past being able to sleep but could only cry to herself in the darkness.

The contrast between her life in the great mansion owned by her uncle and that in the small Manor House where she had lived with her father and mother was like being propelled out of Heaven into an indescribable hell.

At times she had even contemplated drowning herself in the lake or shooting herself with one of her uncle's duelling-pistols.

Then pride made her tell herself that she would not be broken by people she not only hated but despised.

Everything about her uncle, she thought, was different from the kindness, sympathy, and understanding of her mother.

She knew that her father had never liked him and was only too glad that Sir Aylmer preferred to ignore his brother-in-law's very existence because he considered him poor and unimportant.

This morning had come breaking-point.

She had been beaten because Niobe was, although she would not admit it, slightly nervous at having to tell the Viscount she would not marry him, and her uncle had found that the Marquis of Porthcawl's Lawyer would not agree to everything he wished incorporated in the marriage-settlement.

There was one person about the house who always bore the brunt of their temper, and that was Jemima, and she had been unfortunate enough to inadvertently knock over a small table on which was standing a china figure.

It was unlike her to be clumsy, but one of Sir Aylmer's dogs, rushing towards him when he entered the house, had nearly knocked her off her feet and as she stumbled she caught at the table and it fell to the ground.

Sir Aylmer had a riding-whip in his hand, which he straightaway used on her, and as Jemima dragged herself upstairs not only feeling faint from the pain but sick because there was nothing she could do to protect herself, she had known that she must run away.

She was aware that the Viscount was to call on Niobe after luncheon, and when she had come downstairs to attend to the many duties that waited for her, which if left undone would once again bring down her uncle's wrath upon her head, she had seen his Phaeton outside the open front door.

She saw that he had come without a groom and there was only Jeb at the heads of the horses, a stable-boy who was not very bright in other ways but who was good with animals.

Quite suddenly a plan of escape had formed in Jemima's mind.

When she reached the Hall, she saw surprisingly that there were no footmen in attendance and she supposed they were still clearing up after the house-party which had filled the house for the Ball and had left during the morning.

Without really having time to think, knowing that she must act, she had run to the huge carved oak settle in the Hall where the carriage-rugs were kept, and, taking one out, she had slipped out the front door and down the steps to the Phaeton, seeing as she did so that Jeb, occupied in patting the horses, had not noticed her.

She had climbed into the Phaeton on the off-side and covered herself with the rugs. Then, with her heart beating wildly and her lips dry from sheer fear, she had waited.

Now she was free.

As she dressed herself quickly, having learnt from the maid before she left the room that the Viscount was downstairs having breakfast, it flashed through Jemima's mind that she might have changed one task-master for another.

She had seen the Viscount innumerable times when he had called on Niobe either in London or in the country, and she had always thought he was not only the most handsome of her cousin's suitors but certainly sounded the most pleasant.

She had never met him, but then she was not allowed to meet any of Niobe's friends.

She could only admit to watching them when they were not aware of it, simply because she found it an interesting spectacle although she thought at times they were rather like animals in a menagerie.

In London she had peeped through the bannisters and watched the guests who came to the huge dinner-parties which her uncle gave.

In the country there was a Minstrel's Gallery in the great Baronial Dining-Room with a carved oak screen from behind which she could see but remain invisible.

When the family was alone she ate with them, but it usually ended with both Sir Aylmer and Niobe finding fault with her.

She therefore much preferred to have meals in the Morning-Room, where she wrote Niobe's letters for her, addressed invitations for the parties, and helped Sir Aylmer's Secretary, who was always overworked.

Now, looking at the man who suddenly, unexpectedly, and incredibly was her husband, she wondered what her life would be like in the future and how different it would be from the one she had been able to stand no longer.

The Viscount finished writing the notice for the *Gazette* and rose to his feet.

"I will take this to my Club," he said, "and have the Porter take it from there. You had better go to bed."

Jemima rose too.

"Perhaps," she said in a hesitating little voice, "someone . . . would show me where . . . I am to . . . sleep."

"Yes, of course, the Housekeeper can do that."

He tugged at the bell with his hand.

"W-would it be . . . possible," Jemima asked, "if it is no trouble . . . for me to have . . . something to . . . eat?"

"You are hungry?" the Viscount asked, as if it were a surprising thing to be.

"I did not have any breakfast."

Jemima did not bother to explain that she had also missed luncheon because she had been crying from the beating she had endured.

It was only now that she felt empty inside and exhausted, and she was sure it was from lack of food.

The door opened.

"Miss . . ." the Viscount began, then corrected himself: "Her Ladyship requires something to eat, and tell your wife to show her where she can sleep."

"The lady's staying here?"

The man was naturally surprised. At the same time, Jemima thought, there was something slightly impertinent in the way the Butler asked the question.

"This is my wife, Kingston," the Viscount announced, "and your new mistress!"

As he spoke, he walked out of the Library, leaving the Butler staring after him with his mouth open.

There was the sound of the door slamming. Then the Butler looked at Jemima to say, again in a somewhat impertinent manner:

"Do I understand His Lordship aright? He's married you?"

Jemima lifted her chin.

"You heard what he said," she replied, "and I should be grateful if you would ask your wife to show me the way to my bedroom. I am sure it would be more convenient for me to have something to eat on a tray."

"I don't know about that," the Butler said, "the Chef's gone out, and there were no orders this morning for dinner."

"I am sorry it is inconvenient," Jemima replied, "but if there is nothing else, I would be grateful for some bread and cheese."

"I don't know who's going to get it for you. The Chef don't like us touching the food."

Jemima looked at the man and realised something she had not noticed before. He had been drinking.

He was certainly not the type of servant that her uncle would have employed and she was surprised that the Viscount should have done so.

Then she remembered something that had been

stressed over and over again in her conversations with Niobe about the rival suitors for her hand.

"I like Valient Ockley," she had said reflectively. "He is handsome, and we would be an amazing pair—everybody has said so! But he has no money."

"Why should that worry you?" Jemima asked. "After all, you are very rich."

"I do not wish to spend everything I have on any man, whoever he may be," Niobe had replied. "Besides, Papa says his family house wants thousands and thousands spent on it."

Jemima knew how rich her uncle was and that Niobe already had a huge fortune of her own, and she wondered how it could matter.

"While the Marquis's house," Niobe was saying, "is in perfect condition. In fact Papa says it is exactly what a nobleman's house should look like."

"But the Marquis is old," Jemima said, "and I think he is horrid!"

"When did you see him?" Niobe asked sharply.

"I watched him arrive last night," Jemima answered, "and when he came into the Hall there seemed to be something almost vacant in his expression. I am sure he is a very stupid man."

"You know nothing about it," Niobe snapped. "He is rich, he is a Marquis, and what does it matter if he has been married before."

"His wife is dead?" Jemima asked.

"Of course she is dead," Niobe snapped. "How could I marry him if she were not? And think of my position as the Marchioness of Porthcawl!"

"But ... he would be your husband," Jemima

objected in a whisper. "He would . . . kiss you . . . and I suppose you would sleep in the same bed."

"Really, Jemima! I do not think you should speak of such intimate things!" Niobe answered.

"Until you met the Marquis you always said you loved the Viscount."

For once Niobe's blue eyes seemed to soften.

"I do love him," she said with a little sigh, "and I like him kissing me, I like feeling his arms about me. But a Marquis is much more important than a Viscount."

There was no doubt, Jemima thought later, that the Viscount was not only poor but very badly served.

A rather slovenly woman who was not in the least Jemima's idea of a Housekeeper grudgingly showed her to a bedroom and said sourly that she supposed she ought to occupy it if it was true that the Master had married her.

"I assure you we were married today in the country," Jemima replied.

"Then this is the best room and it's next to his, so I suppose you'd better have it. I hears you want something to eat."

"I would be very grateful for anything," Jemima said. "I am very hungry."

What she finally received was a piece of cold mutton, not well cooked in the first place, which had been slapped on a plate with three cold potatoes.

There was, however, some bread that was comparatively fresh and butter on a dish that wanted cleaning, but Jemima was past being particular.

She ate enough to take away the pangs of hunger. Then as Mrs. Kingston had disappeared and there was apparently nobody to take her tray, she put it outside the door, undressed, and got into bed.

She did not miss the fact that the sheets were torn and had been badly laundered, and the water which stood in the china ewer in her room had a film of dust on it.

But at least, she thought, as she settled herself, careful not to hurt her aching and scarred back, she was out of reach of her uncle and Niobe, and nothing else was of any account.

*   *   *

As she was going down the stairs wearing the same gown in which she had travelled to London, Jemima wondered if the Viscount was already having breakfast and regretting his impulsive action in marrying her.

She supposed that if she had behaved correctly, she should have refused to allow him to do anything so absurd in his desire for revenge.

At the same time, she had known that, whatever his motive in marrying her, from her point of view it was a piece of incredible good fortune, although even now it was hard to appreciate the full significance of it.

She need no longer fear her uncle's cruelty; she was the Viscountess Ockley, and whatever happened in the future, even if the Viscount cast her away with no wish ever to see her again, at least she had a name of which she could be proud.

When the Viscount had first pursued Niobe she had been fascinated not only by him but by his aristrocratic lineage.

"The Ockleys are of real importance," Niobe had said a dozen times. "Hostesses who would never accept Papa, because he is only a Knight and has made his fortune rather than inherited it, will never close their doors to an Ockley."

Now while Jemima felt a sense of elation at bearing the Viscount's name, she was still nervous as to what sort of mood he would be in.

She was wondering where to find the Dining-Room, for there was nobody in the Hall to tell her, when she heard voices and went in the direction from which they came.

The Viscount had in fact come downstairs with a thick head which he knew was due to the amount of claret he had consumed last night.

If there was one thing he really disliked, it was suffering from the effects of over-indulgence in drink, because in that particular he was normally very abstemious.

Because he wished to ride as a light-weight in the races and Steeple-Chases which he and his friends organised, he neither ate nor drank more than he considered necessary to keep himself in good health.

But last night, after he had sent the notice of his marriage to the *Gazette,* he had found a number of friends at White's Club and had surprised them by the amount of claret he consumed before finally in the early hours of the morning they all staggered home to bed.

The Viscount had decided that he would not tell anyone he was married until the announcement appeared the following morning.

"I will let it be a surprise," he decided, and knew

with satisfaction that it would certainly be a very
unpleasant surprise for Niobe.

The more he thought of her behaviour and remembered that Jemima had confirmed what he had
already suspected—that she had kept him dangling
until she was quite certain Porthcawl was "in the
bag"—the angrier he grew.

He had sat, drinking, listening to his friends but
not joining in the conversation as he usually did,
until one after the other they asked him what was
the matter. 2111568

When he did not reply, they looked at one another knowingly, certain that he had been turned
down by Niobe Barrington.

It was only Freddy, because he was so close to
the Viscount, who had the temerity to ask the question which hovered on all their lips as he offered
him a lift in his carriage.

"I know you went to the country today, Valient,"
he said. "Did she refuse you?"

"I have no wish to discuss it," the Viscount answered truculently, slurring his speech a little. "Tell
you about it tomorrow, Freddy. Have breakfast
with me."

"I will do that," Freddy replied. "I am sorry, old
chap, if what I suspect has happened, but she is not
the only heiress in the world by a long chalk."

He meant to sound sympathetic, but the Viscount
merely uttered an oath under his breath and left
without saying good-night.

Freddy sat back in his comfortable carriage and
as it drove on he said to himself:

"Poor old Valient! He is taking it hard! I had a

feeling she would prefer a Marquis's coronet. What woman could resist one?"

* * *

The Viscount had no sooner reached the Dining-Room and was lifting the lid of a silver dish which was badly in need of cleaning, to see what it contained, when Freddy walked in unannounced.

"Good-morning, Valient," he said in what the Viscount thought was an over-hearty voice. "I hope you are in a better mood this morning."

"If you want the truth, I feel damned ill," the Viscount replied, dropping the lid of the entree dish with a clatter.

"I am not surprised," Freddy answered. "You must have drunk at least three bottles last night!"

The Viscount groaned and poured himself a cup of black coffee.

Freddy settled himself in a chair and opened the newspaper he had brought in with him under his arm.

"Have you seen the news?" he asked. "The farmers are making a noisy complaint about the competition of cheap imported food entering the country."

He turned the pages and exclaimed:

"Good God!"

There was silence as he read again what had surprised him. Then he said:

"She's accepted you! Why on earth did you not tell me? You must have known it last night."

He glanced at the paper as if he could hardly believe his eyes, and repeated:

"She has accepted you! But the newspaper has got it wrong! They say you are married!"

"Read it to me!" the Viscount ordered.

"It seems extraordinary that they have made a mistake like this!" Freddy answered. "What is written here is: 'The marriage took place quietly yesterday between the fifth Viscount Ockley, of Ockley Hall, Northamptonshire, and Miss Barrington.'"

"Very accurate," the Viscount approved.

Freddy stared at him in astonishment, but before he could ask for an explanation the door opened and Jemima came into the Dining-Room.

Freddy turned his head to look at her. Then as he rose to his feet the Viscount said:

"Good-morning, Jemima. May I present my friend Frederick Hinlip? Freddy, this is my wife, who was Jemima Barrington!"

For a moment Freddy was completely speechless.

For the first time the darkness in the Viscount's eyes seemed to lighten and he looked cynically amused.

"I am so sorry I am late," Jemima apologised, "but I overslept. Something I have not been able to do for a long time."

"There was no hurry," the Viscount said. "You will find some food on the sideboard, but it is not very appetising."

"I am afraid I am still hungry," Jemima said with a smile.

The Viscount had the grace to look a little embarrassed.

"Did Kingston not bring you anything last night?"

"Yes, he brought me what there was, but he said the Chef was out."

Freddy recovered his voice.

"Is this some sort of joke?" he asked.

"Certainly not!" the Viscount replied. "If you want the truth, Freddy, and it is not to be repeated to anybody else, Niobe has accepted Porthcawl, and her cousin Jemima had a burning desire, for which I do not blame her, to rid herself of her uncle's hospitality."

Freddy was staring at his friend with shrewd eyes.

"So you thought you would put one over on Niobe?"

"I have always said that you are quick on the uptake, Freddy," the Viscount remarked. "You are right. That is exactly what I have done! I am just wondering how long it will take for the gossips in the Clubs to find out that the Barrington I have married is not the Barrington they expected."

"You certainly do things in a very strange way."

Freddy looked a little critically at Jemima as she came from the sideboard carrying a plate on which there were two poached eggs and some slices of bacon.

Once again he rose halfway to his feet as she seated herself at the table.

Then as she gave a rather shy little smile, he told himself that she was attractive or rather he could have thought so if he had not expected her to be her cousin.

Aloud he said:

"So you are married, and of course I must congratulate you both. Now what are you going to do?"

"Do?" the Viscount enquired. "What do you expect us to do?"

"I was just wondering," Freddy answered, "why

I have not had the pleasure of meeting Her Lady-ship before."

"I was not allowed to attend the dinner-parties to which you were invited, Mr. Hinlip," Jemima replied. "You see, I am only the poor relation."

"The poor relation?" Freddy repeated.

"Very poor," Jemima confirmed. "My entire fortune, as His Lordship knows, is two guineas!"

Once again Freddy looked astonished, and the Viscount said:

"It is obviously not to be repeated, but Jemima was running away and was coming to London with nowhere to go and only that amount of money in her purse."

"Good Lord!" Freddy exclaimed. "You were certainly a Knight to the rescue, whatever other motives you may have had for such a precipitate marriage."

"I am very, very grateful," Jemima said, "but I was afraid that this morning you would be regretting your kindness to me."

She looked across the table at the Viscount as she spoke, and she had the feeling as her eyes met his that he was looking at her for the first time.

As if Freddy was suddenly aware that the two people to whom he was talking were married, he said:

"I expect you want to be alone, and I imagine, Valient, you will not be accompanying me to the Mill at Hampstead Heath as we had planned."

"Of course I am coming to the Mill!" the Viscount said quickly. "I am convinced that Sergeant Jenkins will win, and I intend to put my money on him."

Freddy looked from the Viscount to Jemima.

"What about Her Ladyship?"

"Oh, please, could I come too?" Jemima enquired. "I would love to see a Mill. In fact I have always wanted to see one!"

"Ladies never attend Mills," the Viscount replied.

"But I am not..." Jemima began, then said hastily, "but I suppose I am ... now. I find it hard to ... remember."

"It would certainly be a mistake," Freddy said when the Viscount did not speak, "to appear in public for the first time at a Mill."

He looked at the Viscount as he said:

"You must be aware, Valient, that everybody will be agog to see your wife. I imagine by this time the place will be a-buzz with speculation as to how you managed to beat Porthcawl at the post, and when it is learnt that you have married someone other than Niobe Barrington, they will be consumed with curiosity."

"Of course they will be curious, and a good thing, too," the Viscount said. "Nothing will annoy Niobe more."

"That is true," Jemima said, "and she will be very ... angry. But, please, may I suggest something?"

"Yes, of course," the Viscount replied.

"It is just," Jemima said, and the colour rose in her face, "that I came away ... just as I was ... bringing nothing with me."

"Nothing!" Freddy exclaimed.

"It was only as I came down the stairs after Uncle Aylmer had beaten me that I knew I could not ... stand it any ... more."

"Are you saying Sir Aylmer beat you? It is not possible!" Freddy said.

"That is what His Lordship said," Jemima replied, "and I know he thought I was making it up ... but look!"

She turned round as she spoke, and as her gown, which had belonged to Niobe but had always been too big for her, was cut rather low at the back, both men could see several large weals on her white skin.

As they stared at the marks incredulously, Jemima turned back and said:

"They are much worse lower down, but now you know I am not lying."

"It is the most preposterous thing I have ever heard!" Freddy said angrily. "The man must be a monster!"

"I have always disliked him and thought him an outsider," the Viscount added. "But I never imagined he was the type of swine who would be brutal to a young girl!"

He thought as he spoke that Jemima looked little more than a child. In fact she was so small that she might easily have passed for one.

It flashed through his mind that he might be accused of abducting a minor without her Guardian's consent.

Then he told himself that the one thing Sir Aylmer would not want was the type of publicity which would inform the Social World of the repulsive manner in which he had treated a relative who was dependent upon him.

"I was thinking," Freddy said after what seemed to be a long pause, "that as Her Ladyship is—"

"Oh, for Heaven's sake, Freddy, call her Jemima!" the Viscount interrupted. "I keep thinking you are talking about my mother!"

"Very well; as Jemima has to buy some clothes anyway, she might as well have a trousseau that will make her appear the sort of girl you preferred to Niobe."

Both the Viscount and Jemima understood immediately what he was trying to say tactfully, so as not to hurt her feelings.

"Could I really have some new clothes that are pretty, and are made for me?" she asked. "I have had only Niobe's cast-offs for the last two years, and however well I tried to alter them, they always looked wrong on me. Besides, I am dark, and I know Mama always said that pastel shades did not suit me."

"Go and buy as many gowns as you like," the Viscount said, "and you had better shop at Madame Bertha's. I owe her a large amount already!"

"You owe Madame Bertha money?" Jemima asked in astonishment.

Then the puzzled look went from her face and she gave a little laugh.

"But of course! How stupid of me. I was thinking it was strange for you to have an account with a fashionable dressmaker, but that is where you must have bought things for the 'bits o' muslin' you have fancied."

"Good God! You must not say things like that!" the Viscount said sharply.

There was so much surprise in his voice and on Freddy's face that Jemima blushed.

"I am . . . sorry," she said quickly. "Was that . . . wrong?"

"Of course it was wrong," the Viscount said. "You should not even know about 'bits o' muslin,' let alone use that particular expression. I cannot believe your uncle . . . ."

"No, it was not Uncle Aylmer who talked about them," Jemima said, "but a distant cousin, Oliver Barrington."

"A very unpleasant chap, Oliver Barrington!" Freddy remarked. "I never could stand him when we were at School together."

"I agree with you," the Viscount said. "In the future you had better forget anything he said to you."

"Oh, he did not say it to me," Jemima replied, "but just as people always think servants are deaf and dumb and therefore talk indiscreetly in front of them, so poor relations are in the same category."

Freddy laughed as if he could not help it. Then he said:

"You have to forget that you are a poor relation. That is not at all the type of lineage that Valient wants to produce in his wife. You are a niece of Sir Aylmer—although God help you—and you will hold your head high and make everyone think that by sheer cleverness Valient has found a wife in a million."

Jemima looked at him with big eyes and said in a very small voice:

"You . . . really think I can . . . do that?"

"It is something you have to do," Freddy said. "Valient has got himself into this . . . ."

He changed the word "mess" as it actually reached his lips and substituted "position."

"And it is important that he does not have Porthcawl and for that matter Niobe laughing at him."

"No, no! Of course not! I understand!" Jemima said. "Perhaps it would be . . . better if I went away . . disappeared."

She made a little sound that was almost a sob as she said:

"I see now it was . . . wrong of me to agree to marry you . . . but at the time it seemed so wonderful that you should . . . help me just at the moment when I was almost in . . . despair."

"I am glad I was able to help you," the Viscount said in a determined voice, as if he wanted to convince himself. "And Freddy is right—we have to put a good face on it, and not creep about like beaten dogs with our tails between our legs."

"That is the spirit!" Freddy approved. "And it is up to Jemima."

He looked at her from the other side of the table and she knew he was studying her, taking in her good points.

"I will do anything you want me to do," she said, "but I am well aware I cannot compare with Niobe."

"I remember once," Freddy said, "asking my mother whom she loved best, my brother or me, and she picked two flowers from the garden before she answered. One of them was a rose and the other was a lily, and she said to me:

" 'Which do you think is the more beautiful of these two flowers?'

"I answered: 'I do not know, Mama, they are both very lovely in their different ways.'

" 'Exactly!' she said. 'You cannot compare them one with the other. You can only admire them both, and that is what I feel about you and Charlie. You are two different people, and I admire and love you because you are my sons. There is no question of first or second, but just two boys who are equally adored.' "

"What a wonderful answer!" Jemima said. "I shall remember that in case, when I have children, they ask the same question."

Then as if she realised what she had said, she looked a little shy and added quickly:

"I will try to look my very, very best, and perhaps if I have pretty gowns and my hair is done fashionably His Lordship will not be ashamed of me."

"I have no intention of being anything but proud of you," the Viscount said, again in a voice which sounded forced.

There was a little pause, then Jemima said:

"Then ... please ... could you come with me and help me choose the right gowns? I do not think I could ... manage by myself."

The Viscount looked surprised, but Freddy laughed.

"Why not, Valient? You have good taste when you want to use it, as I remember noticing on several occasions in the past."

"Be quiet!" the Viscount said hastily. "You are worse than Oliver Barrington!"

"I hope not," Freddy said, "but I do not mind admitting that when my sisters want to 'cut a dash,' they often parade their gowns in front of me for me to decide which they should buy."

"Very well," the Viscount decided, "we will go shopping with Jemima."

"Not as she is looking now," Freddy said quickly.

"Why not?" the Viscount enquired.

"Because," Freddy said, "it will be all over London within half-an-hour of our entering Madame Bertha's shop that she was not—forgive me, Jemima—up to snuff."

Jemima knew exactly what he meant. The gown she was wearing had been creased by her sitting on the floor of the Phaeton covered with the rug, and it was still creased although she had hung it carefully in the wardrobe when she had taken it off.

What was more, not only did it not fit her, because although she had altered it several times it was still too big, but the pale "love-in-a-mist" blue which looked entrancing on Niobe merely made Jemima's skin look sallow.

Moreover, her hair, which she washed herself, curled over her head without being styled or fashionably arranged.

There had never been time for her to do much about it, and even so she was quite certain that if she had appeared looking fashionable, her looks would have annoyed Niobe more than they did already.

She had therefore let it flow as nature intended, and now as she put up a nervous little hand as if to put it into place, she was aware what a hobbledehoy she must look in the eyes not only of Mr. Hinlip but also of the Viscount.

"What we will do," Freddy said now, "is send

my carriage to Bond Street to bring back Madame
Bertha with some gowns for Jemima to wear immediately. Then we will go shopping, and if you
are not the producer of a Prima-Donna, Valient, I
am!"

Jemima clapped her hands.

"That would be wonderful . . . wonderful!" she
said. "But what about the Mill?"

"It is not until two o'clock," Freddy said. "It
should not take us more than three-quarters-of-an-
hour to reach Wimbledon Common, and we can
buy you quite a few rags by that time."

Jemima knew he was speaking jestingly.

But it was the most thrilling thing that had ever
happened, when, two hours later, dressed in a
strawberry-pink muslin trimmed with lace and
wearing a bonnet decorated with flowers of the
same colour, she drove with the Viscount and
Freddy to Bond Street.

They visited not only Madame Bertha's shop to
see some gowns which she had not brought to
Berkeley Square, but several other dressmakers at
which either the Viscount or Freddy was well
known.

When Jemima was introduced as the new Viscountess, the proprietress was all smiles and eager-
ness to please, and when at a quarter-to-one Freddy
said it was time for them to drop Jemima at Berkeley Square and set off for Wimbledon, she thought
breathlessly that no girl, except one in a fairy-tale,
could ever have had a trousseau provided at such
an unprecedented speed.

When they turned in to the Square, Freddy said:
"There will be a lot of other things you will

want, such as sunshades, shoes, gloves, the whole caboodle, and I suggest you buy those yourself this afternoon. But you must not go alone."

"Who can I take with me?" Jemima enquired.

"I suppose one of your servants could accompany her?" Freddy asked the Viscount.

"Perhaps I could take the maid who called me," Jemima suggested quickly. "She seemed a nice girl."

"I expect she will do," the Viscount said in an uninterested voice.

"Thank you ... thank you very much for saying I may buy what I want," Jemima said, "and thank you a thousand times for all the wonderful things you have given me this morning. I never thought ... I never dreamt I would own such beautiful gowns!"

"I am sure you will look fine in them," the Viscount said in the same voice he had used before, and it was Freddy who noticed the look of disappointment in her eyes.

"I tell you what we will do," he said. "I expect we shall do some celebrating when the fight is over, and why should we not dine with you tonight, Valient? I am sure if you invite them quite a number of our friends would be only too delighted to have an opportunity of meeting Jemima."

"All right," the Viscount agreed. "Tell Kingston that we shall be at least ten for dinner and I expect the Chef to provide something worth eating."

"I will tell him," Jemima replied.

She had already been helped out of the Phaeton by Freddy, as the Viscount was driving the horses and was unable to move.

"Wear your prettiest gown, Jemima," he said in a low voice, "and remember it is very important that Valient's friends should be impressed by you."

"I shall not forget that," Jemima answered nervously.

Freddy squeezed her hand, then climbed into the Phaeton.

As they drove off he turned back to see her standing on the top step, looking small, smart, but rather forlorn, and as he waved she waved back.

"You know, Valient," he said as they drove away, "there is no doubt that you have the luck of the devil!"

Chapter Three

As the Phaeton disappeared round the Square, Jemima walked into the Hall and as she did so the Viscount's valet Hawkins came running from under the stairs.

He was a short, wiry little man with the obvious stamp of a soldier on him, who had been the Viscount's batman ever since he had joined the Regiment, and he had retired with him into civilian life.

"Has His Lordship left?" he asked Jemima breathlessly.

"Yes, he and Mr. Hinlip have gone to a Mill on Wimbledon Common," Jemima replied.

She knew who Hawkins was because she had noticed him last night when Mrs. Kingston was escorting her, with a bad grace, to her bedroom.

Hawkins muttered something under his breath and Jemima asked:

"Is anything wrong?"

"Yes, indeed, M'Lady," the valet replied, "and I'm not sure what I should do about it."

"Perhaps I could help," Jemima suggested.

She thought Hawkins looked embarrassed before he said:

"Well, it's like this, M'Lady, the staff's leaving."

"Leaving!" Jemima exclaimed. "But why?"

There was a pause before Hawkins said uncomfortably:

"They don't like the idea of the Master being married."

Jemima looked at him in consternation.

"I have no wish to cause trouble."

At the same time, she thought of the dust in the Sitting-Room, the condition of the sheets, and the meal she had been given last night, and she felt that the Kingstons would really be no loss.

But as she was not certain what the Viscount would feel, she said quickly:

"I will come and speak to them. I am sure when I tell them I have no wish to interfere they will stay. Perhaps you will show me the way to the kitchen."

"Of course, M'Lady," Hawkins agreed.

She had the feeling, although there was no reason for it, that he had the same opinion of the Kingstons as she had.

They went along the passage and down some back stairs which obviously needed cleaning.

A flagged floor in the basement which could not have been scrubbed for months took them towards the kitchen.

Then as they passed the Pantry, Jemima glanced towards it and saw the glint of something which shone sticking out of a leather bag.

She paused, and as she did so, Kingston ap-

peared from a large safe, carrying a silver candlestick in his hand.

Jemima walked into the Pantry.

"I understand, Kingston," she said in a voice
that sounded more courageous than she felt, "that
you and your wife are leaving His Lordship's employment."

She saw that Kingston was surprised to see her,
and he quickly put the candlestick he was holding
back in the safe before he replied in a surly tone:

"We're engaged t' work for a single gentleman."

"I can understand your dissatisfaction," Jemima
replied, "but naturally you will be expected to work
out your notice before you leave."

"We're goin' now!" Kingston said derisively.
"And we wants th' wages to which we're entitled."

Jemima looked down at the black bag, saw that
the glint of silver she had seen through the doorway
came from the base of a candlestick that was the
pair of the one which he had taken from the safe,
and said:

"I imagine you are taking the candlestick that I
see in that bag to be mended. But, as you are leaving, I will see to it, so please put it back in the
safe."

There was a moment's pregnant silence and she
thought that Kingston was about to defy her. Then
Hawkins, who had been standing outside in the
passage, came into the Pantry and Kingston capitu-
lated.

"That's true, M'Lady. I were havin' them
mended," he said, "but as I suspected, you'll be
fault-finding an' interfering, and I'm not staying to
listen to that."

"You'll keep a civil tongue in your head," Hawkins said sharply, "and speak to Her Ladyship respectful-like!"

Kingston was defeated and he knew it.

He took the candlestick out of the bag and Jemima saw that underneath it were several attractive comfit-dishes.

She did not say anything, she only looked until the bag was empty, and Hawkins stepped forward to shut the safe door, lock it, and hand the key to her.

"Thank you, Hawkins," she said.

He knew that she thanked him not only for the key but also for his support, and as she walked from the Pantry she heard him say:

"The sooner you get out of here, th' better, or I'll inform against you in front of th' Magistrates."

Kingston replied with a dirty word which Jemima pretended she had not heard, and she walked on in the direction of what she knew was the kitchen.

Hawkins caught up with her as she reached the door.

Mrs. Kingston was inside, already dressed in a bonnet and shawl, and a number of packages were heaped on the kitchen-table beside the remains of a meal.

Mrs. Kingston took one look at Jemima and would have been exceedingly rude if Hawkins had not prevented her by saying:

"You're not leaving until you've opened these parcels an' showed Her Ladyship what's inside. We've just caught your husband nicking th' silver candlesticks."

Mrs. Kingston gave a gasp and Hawkins went on:

"You knows th' penalty for stealing as well as I do—hanging or transportation for anything that's worth more than a shilling!"

Mrs. Kingston let out a scream, and, picking up a wicker-basket which must have contained her clothes, she pushed past Hawkins and was out of the kitchen-door and down the passage before he could say any more.

They heard her shouting for her husband. Then there was the sound of the back door slamming and after that silence.

"Well, they've gone!" Hawkins said. "And if you asks me, M'Lady, it's good riddance to bad rubbish!"

"I rather thought that myself," Jemima replied, "but I have no wish to upset His Lordship."

"Them Kingstons have been drinking his wine, an' half the money His Lordship gave the Chef for food has been divided amongst the three of 'em."

"Where is the Chef now?" Jemima enquired.

"He left an hour ago," Hawkins replied. "He were afraid Your Ladyship would find out what he'd been up to."

"Why did you not tell His Lordship they were cheating him?" Jemima enquired.

Hawkins thought for a moment, then he said:

"It's like this, M'Lady. In the Army we lives an' lets live. If His Lordship had asked me I'd have told him th' truth, but as long as things jogged along, so to speak, I thinks there wasn't any point stirring up trouble."

"I can understand that," Jemima said. "Now,

suppose we see what they were taking away with them."

They opened the packages on the table and found that they contained all sorts of small objects that had been collected round the house, some of which were valuable, some mere trinkets, but Jemima felt glad that they had been saved from the thieving hands of the Kingstons.

Only when they had put everything they had unpacked onto a tray to be carried back to their rightful places did Jemima remember the message the Viscount had given her.

"What are we to do, Hawkins?" she asked. "His Lordship has said we will be at least ten for dinner tonight."

"I doubts if we can get servants from th' Bureau as quick as that," Hawkins answered.

There was a pause, then Jemima said:

"Then I will tell you what we must do . . ."

* * *

The Viscount came back from the Mill in an exceedingly good humour.

Not only had he enjoyed the Mill itself and watched the Sergeant he had backed beating his opponent, a Bombardier, into a pulp, in twenty-six rounds, but he had also been cynically amused by the congratulations he had received from his friends and acquaintances.

He found himself wondering if they would have been so effusive if they had been thinking only of Niobe's beauty rather than her great fortune.

The general attitude was that he had been exceedingly clever and had pulled off a coup for which he could be justifiably envied.

In fact, after the Mill was over, if he had drunk with his friends and everyone else who wished to toast his future happiness, he would have been quite incapable of driving Freddy's horses.

Because Freddy was prepared to acknowledge that the Viscount tooled the reins better than he did, he preferred to let his friend drive rather, as he had often said, than have him finding fault.

While the Viscount was completely sober, the fact that he had got away with his deception made him feel the same elation as a mischievous young boy who had stolen a farmer's best apples without being caught.

"How long are you going to keep up this farce?" Freddy asked as they started for home.

"Until they learn the truth," the Viscount replied.

"They will be damned angry when they realise you have made fools of them."

"What can they say?" the Viscount enquired. "I have married a Miss Barrington, I have never for one moment lied, or said that her name was Niobe. I only wish I could have been a fly on the wall this morning, to hear what she and Sir Aylmer had to say about it!"

"The trouble with you is that you are becoming sadistic in your old age!"

"She played me a dirty trick and she deserves one in return," the Viscount said in an uncompromising tone.

"I am inclined to agree with you," Freddy replied. "At the same time, I cannot help feeling, Valient, that you are skating on very thin ice."

The Viscount did not reply for a moment. Then he said:

"We will see what happens tonight. You realise whom I have asked to dinner?"

"I was in fact rather surprised at your choice."

"Alvanley is the greatest gossip in London," the Viscount said, "and if he approves of Jemima the rest will follow suit. Chesham is a lady's-man, and I have never known him to resist a pretty face."

Freddy did not reply, and after a moment the Viscount said:

"I know what you are thinking, but as it happens Chesham dislikes Niobe."

"Why?"

"She slapped him down apparently before she knew how important he was. Afterwards when she tried to suck up to him he would have none of it."

"That sounds very like her," Freddy said, "and if you ask my opinion, Valient, the more I hear about Niobe and her father, the more convinced I am that you should be grateful for being rid of them rather than seeking any sort of revenge."

"We look at things differently," the Viscount said crushingly, and Freddy said no more.

The Viscount was in fact very late getting back to the house in Berkeley Square, for the simple reason that he could not resist dropping into White's for a few minutes just to hear what the members had to say about his marriage.

Some of them he had already seen at the Mill. The rest, who had spent the afternoon gossipping in the leather-covered Club chairs, had a great deal to say on the subject.

It was only when Freddy looked pointedly at his watch that the Viscount managed to tear himself away and set off at great speed for Berkeley Square.

"I hope to God the Chef has made a proper effort for once," he said just before he drew his horses to a standstill.

"You might have waited until Jemima had taken her place as mistress of the house," Freddy remarked.

"Jemima? I doubt if she has any idea of running one," the Viscount replied. "Besides, by that time it will be too late."

They both knew what he meant and Freddy merely grinned and said:

"See that the wine is up to scratch. That always covers a multitude of sins."

As the horses came to a standstill Freddy took the reins and the Viscount hurried up the steps to find not Kingston but Hawkins waiting at the door.

"All right, Hawkins," he said, "I know I am late, but I expect you have everything ready for me."

He did not wait for an answer but went up the stairs two at a time to find, as he had expected, that his bath was drawn and his clothes were laid out on the bed.

If Hawkins was slightly less attentive than usual the Viscount did not notice, because he was still thinking of the congratulations he had received at the Mill and at the Club.

He was also wondering what Lord Alvanley, Lord Chesham, and the other men he had invited to dinner would think when they met Jemima instead of Niobe.

They would consider it strange, for one thing, that he was giving a dinner-party the second night of their honeymoon.

However, his guests had been flattered to be asked and he was sure they were already boasting to their friends that they would be the first to congratulate and doubtless to kiss the bride.

The Viscount had cut it so fine that as he came down the stairs with his crisp white cravat tied meticulously and his long-tailed evening-coat fitting over the shoulders in a manner which could only have been achieved by Weston, he saw Lord Alvanley followed by Lord Worcester and Sir Stafford Lumley walking into the Hall.

He greeted them effusively and led them into the Drawing-Room to find to his annoyance that Freddy was already there, having reached his lodgings in Half Moon Street, changed, and returned in shorter time than the Viscount had managed without that journey.

There was no sign of Jemima, and when four more of their guests arrived he was wondering whether he should ask a servant to fetch her, when his valet came to his side to say in a low voice:

"Her Ladyship's apologies, M'Lord, but she's been unavoidably delayed and would be obliged if you'd start dinner without her."

There was a frown between the Viscount's eyes, but he knew it would be a mistake to show his annoyance, so he merely said sharply:

"Tell Her Ladyship to be as quick as possible!" and turned to his guests.

The champagne that had been waiting for them in the ice-coolers had been correctly chilled, and at exactly the right moment dinner was announced.

The Viscount made his wife's apologies before they walked into the Dining-Room.

As the first entree was passed round the table, the Viscount was suddenly aware that his valet and a young housemaid were waiting at table.

He was about to demand to be told what had happened to Kingston, then he thought it would be a mistake to draw attention to any shortcomings in his household, and as the dinner seemed to be proceeding without a hitch he said nothing.

However, he was pleasantly aware some time later that the food was far better than he remembered it ever being before and that Alvanley, who was a known gourmet, has said complimentary things about at least two of the dishes.

Hawkins kept the glasses filled, and there was an air of joviality and good humour about the party, besides the fact that the conversation was, the Viscount thought, unusually witty and stimulating.

The only thing that annoyed him was the empty chair at the other end of the table.

He could not imagine what was keeping Jemima and thought that either her new gown had not arrived or she had had an attack of shyness, which seemed on consideration somewhat unlikely.

Finally, as a dessert of large peaches and muscat grapes was placed on the table, and a china bowl filled with nuts with which to accompany the port, the door opened and Jemima came into the room.

The Viscount saw her first and rose to his feet, and as his guests turned their heads and rose too, he thought with satisfaction that she was looking extremely attractive.

He had chosen her gown himself and therefore her appearance owed nothing to Freddy, but it was a choice with which it would have been difficult to quarrel.

The crimson of her dress, which was ornamented with ruchings of tulle round the shoulders and the hem, besides some expensive diamanté embroidery, made her skin seem almost dazzlingly white.

Because she was apprehensive and perhaps, although she would not have acknowledged it, embarrassed, her eyes seemed unnaturally large in her small face.

Her hair, dressed in the very latest fashion by a hair-dresser procured during the afternoon by Hawkins, seemed to hold mysterious blue lights in it that no-one had ever noticed before.

She came towards the table, and as the Viscount saw the questioning surprise in his guests' eyes, he said:

"My dear, may I present my friends. Gentlemen —my wife!"

He had the satisfaction of hearing quite an audible gasp before Jemima curtseyed and seated herself in the chair at the end of the table which Hawkins held for her.

"I must apologise for being late," Jemima said.

She spoke in a small, musical voice that seemed to break the almost unnatural silence which had heralded the Viscount's announcement.

"I was wondering what kept you," he replied. "I am afraid you have missed a very excellent dinner.

We must certainly congratulate the Chef tomorrow morning."

He thought there was a twinkle in Jemima's eyes, but it might have been a trick of the light, as she replied:

"I hope, My Lord, that you will do that."

Lord Alvanley was brave enough to ask the question which was trembling on everybody's lips.

"There must have been a misprint in this morning's *Gazette,* Ockley," he said, "for I understood from what I read that you had married Miss Barrington."

"The announcement was correct," the Viscount replied laconically, "but as it happens, my wife is Sir Aylmer's niece, Jemima, and not his daughter."

There was no doubt that everybody present, with the exception of Freddy, was astonished, and the Viscount could not help being amused at the manner in which they tried quickly to adjust themselves to the situation.

"I claim the privilege," said Lord Chesham, who was sitting on Jemima's right, "to drink the health of the bride and wish her every happiness, while of course Ockley must receive our unreserved congratulations."

There was no doubt that he spoke with sincerity, and Jemima flashed him a little smile that showed the dimples in her cheeks.

She looked so pretty that the toast that followed was said in all sincerity.

Only Lord Worcester, who was sitting next to the Viscount, put into words what they were all thinking.

"One thing about you, Valient," he said, "is that

you never fail to surprise even your friends, and tonight, like Sergeant Jenkins, you have knocked the breath out of our bodies!"

As the Viscount smiled complacently, Lord Worcester said in a low voice that only he could hear:

"What about Niobe? I was quite certain that she was as infatuated with you as you were with her."

"I have always found it wise to play my cards close to my chest," the Viscount replied.

"It is certainly something you have done in this deal!" Lord Worcester exclaimed. "But I do not blame you. If they had seen her before you, I have no doubt that there would have been a large number of rivals for anyone so fascinating."

"Fascinating" actually was the word most of the guests used in describing Jemima when finally they left the Viscount's house.

In the Drawing-Room they had alternately paid her extravagant compliments and tried vainly to make her explain why she had not appeared in Society until this moment.

It was obvious that all the gentlemen present thought there was some mystery or perhaps a cleverness on the Viscount's part, to have kept her hidden until she actually appeared as his wife.

They were all, Jemima knew, bewildered at finding, as Lord Albany put it, that they had been "barking up the wrong tree" in expecting the Viscount to marry Niobe.

"I cannot think why I did not meet you at your uncle's house," said one man after another. "Or perhaps you did not live there with him?"

"When my parents were alive we lived in Kent," Jemima said evasively.

She tried to parry every question without lying but by avoiding a direct answer, so that when they left, the guests knew as little about her as they had when she first appeared in the Dining-Room.

All they were able to establish was that the Viscount was married but the bride was not who they had expected, but a very charming, friendly, and fascinating little person who listened wide-eyed to everything they said and blushed very prettily at every compliment they paid her.

Some of them had been treated in a very high-handed manner by Niobe after she became spoilt by her success.

It was obvious both to Freddy and to the Viscount that the descriptions they would give of "Ockley's bride" would be very much in her favour.

Only when everybody had left except for Freddy did the Viscount say to Jemima:

"What on earth made you so late for dinner? I began to think you had got a touch of nerves or something."

He did not speak disagreeably, for the simple reason that the evening had gone so well that he was feeling in the same good humour, if not more so, in which he had driven back from the Mill.

Jemima looked at him for a moment, then she said:

"I will wager you one of my precious guineas that you will not guess the reason why I was late."

The Viscount thought for a moment.

"I suppose like all women you took too long to dress, or the hair-dresser did not turn up."

"You speak from experience?"

"I certainly do," the Viscount replied. "Do you remember, Freddy, that little ballet-dancer who was never on . . ."

He stopped suddenly, remembering that Jemima was in a different position, and said abruptly:

"Well, was that the reason?"

"You have lost your money," Jemima answered. "Pay up!"

She put out her hand towards him but the Viscount said:

"Wait a minute! I want to know the reason first."

"Actually," Jemima said, "it was the dinner that kept me."

"The dinner?" the Viscount questioned. "What do you mean? You can hardly have wanted to eat alone? And talking of dinner—what happened to Kingston, and why was Hawkins waiting?"

"That is just what I was going to explain," Jemima answered. "I am afraid the Kingstons have left."

"Left?" the Viscount exclaimed.

"Hawkins and I prevented them from taking the silver candlesticks with them," Jemima said quickly, as if to stop the words which had come to his lips.

"I do not know what you are talking about!" the Viscount exclaimed. "I knew that Kingston drank, but I imagined he was honest."

"You can ask Hawkins about that; and they left because they were frightened that they would not be able to get away with their thieving habits once you were married."

There was an ominous darkness in the Viscount's eyes and Freddy said quickly:

"I always thought Kingston was an unobliging sort of chap, and I imagined he had a partiality for your claret. I am sure Jemima can find you better servants than that."

"I dislike my household being upset," the Viscount said petulantly. "Anyway, the Chef came up to scratch."

"Thank you!" Jemima said. "And now I would be very pleased to listen to the compliments you were ready to pay during dinner."

For a moment both men stared at her as if they could not believe what they had heard.

Freddy spoke first.

"Are you telling us that you cooked the dinner tonight?"

"There was no-one else," Jemima said, "and you must thank Hawkins too. He bought the necessary ingredients in record time. Then I cooked it, and he served it."

For a moment there was absolute silence, then the Viscount began to laugh.

As his laughter rang out in the room Freddy laughed too, and, as if she could not help it, Jemima joined in.

"My God—if they had only known!" the Viscount gasped. "The bride who they thought was the heiress of the year, cooking the food they were stuffing into their mouths, then appearing looking as cool as a cucumber! I hand it to you, Jemima! If I am a trickster, then so are you. They swallowed everything we told them—hook, line, and sinker!"

"How can you cook like that?" Freddy asked when they could speak without laughing.

"My father enjoyed good food," Jemima replied, "and as both Mama and I loved him, we used to study Cookery-Books and surprise him with exotic meals which he always said were as good as anything the Regent's French Chef could serve up at Carlton House."

"I thought the food tonight was better than anything I have eaten in that granite Dining-Room," Freddy replied.

"I still cannot believe it," the Viscount said, "and the only regrettable part of it is that we cannot tell anyone because it would reflect on Jemima."

"You mean on the wife of the Viscount Ockley," Jemima corrected. "I know now that I could have got a position as a cook, if you had not made me a Lady of Quality."

"As far as I am concerned, the two things can be synonymous," the Viscount said. "If you are going to cook like that, why should I need a Chef?"

"What we need at the moment is somebody to clean the kitchens," Jemima said. "Hawkins mopped them down but they need to be scrubbed out properly."

Freddy laughed.

"I imagine tomorrow, instead of buying more objects for your trousseau, you will visit a Domestic Bureau."

"That is what I intend to do," Jemima replied. "There is only one difficulty."

"What is that?" the Viscount enquired.

"Hawkins said that one of the reasons, apart

from me, for the staff being so dissatisfied was that they have not received any wages for some time."

The Viscount looked embarrassed.

"I suppose I have been somewhat remiss over that, but to tell the truth my pockets are to let."

"But surely," Jemima insisted, "we will have to do something about it?"

"I quite agree," the Viscount answered, "but at the moment I am not certain what we can do."

All three of them were suddenly aware that he had been banking on becoming engaged to Niobe, in which case all his financial difficulties would have been over.

Freddy rose to his feet.

"I must be off to bed," he said. "A marvellous evening, Jemima, thanks to you! Valient, you have had the laugh on everybody, especially on one person who aptly deserves it."

The Viscount took him to the door, and when he came back Jemima rose too from the chair in which she was sitting.

"I think I must say good-night," she said. "It has all been very exciting, but rather tiring."

"I want to thank you for a magnificent performance."

"There is no need," Jemima replied, "and if we are to start thanking each other, I am so grateful to you that I do not know where to begin."

As she spoke, she touched her new gown with her fingers as if she could hardly believe she was wearing it.

"You look very different from the little ragamuffin who was hidden under a rug in my Phaeton," the Viscount said with a smile.

"I hope Your Lordship's money has not been wasted," Jemima said demurely.

The Viscount picked up his half-finished glass of brandy and raised it to her.

"Tonight was your success, Jemima—definitely yours!"

She walked towards the door.

"Good-night, My Lord," she said. "I am glad to share in your revenge, or should we change the word to 'triumph'? Breakfast will not be until nine o'clock, as Hawkins has to buy some eggs. We have eaten everything there was in the house!"

Before the Viscount could reply, he heard her footsteps crossing the Hall and knew she was going up the stairs.

'A triumph!' he thought to himself as he drank the remains of his brandy.

Then unpleasantly, almost as if somebody were standing near him, he could hear a voice ask:

"But what of the future? And how, on top of everything else, are you going to pay for a wife?"

*   *   *

Coming back to the house with Emily after a fruitless morning at the Domestic Bureau, Jemima wondered if Hawkins had procured all the things she had wanted for luncheon.

It had taken him a long time to wash down the kitchen and the Pantry. She knew it was a condescension on his part, but he was prepared to do anything which he believed was in the best interests of the Viscount.

She thought to herself that it was easy to judge

the characters of people, especially men, by the devotion they evoked in their servants.

All the servants in her uncle's house had hated him.

Although she would not lower herself to gossip about her cousin, she knew that they disliked Niobe also, for the manner in which she spoke to them and for her insistence that any servant who displeased her would be dismissed without a reference.

It surprised Jemima that the Viscount had engaged the Kingstons in the first place. She had thought he was a better judge of people, for Kingston was not the type of servant she would have expected to find in a nobleman's household.

As they had nearly reached Berkeley Square in the hackney-carriage in which she was driving with Emily, Jemima learnt the explanation.

"I am afraid, Emily," she said, "we are going to have difficulty finding a suitable couple at this particular time of the year. In the Season so many people come up from the country to London that good servants are in great demand."

"That's true enough, M'Lady," Emily agreed, "but His Lordship, poor gentleman, can't pay the prices as them who be well trained demand."

Jemima was startled, then she said:

"Are you saying that His Lordship employed the Kingstons because they were cheap?"

Emily looked embarrassed.

"I would like you to tell me the truth, Emily," Jemima said. "It would in fact be helpful."

"Well, it's like this, M'Lady. When I comes to London I goes to Mrs. Dawson's Agency, being th' best place t' get a situation as a housemaid. I were

told there be three places I could have, an' one of
them was with His Lordship."

She paused before she went on, still looking
rather awkward:

"My parents live on the Ockley Estate in the
country and I'd heard of His Lordship's successes
at the races, since me father always has a flutter
when he's got th' money. So I says to Mrs. Dawson:
'That's where I'd like to go, Ma'am, to th' Viscount
Ockley's.'

" 'If that's your decision it's a very foolish one!'
she says to me, sharp-like. 'His Lordship's a bad
payer, so don't complain later that I didn't warn
you!'

"I was surprised," Emily went on, "thinking as
how gentlemen, especially them with grand titles,
were always rich, but I soon finds out that Mrs.
Dawson's right. Sometimes I gets me wages, an'
sometimes I don't, an' they're less than I could earn
in other houses."

"And yet you stay with His Lordship?" Jemima
asked softly.

"Well, M'Lady, he's ever so handsome, an' perhaps one day his ship'll come in. We all thought it
had when . . ."

Emily suddenly stopped speaking, but Jemima
was well aware what she had been going to say.

For the first time she wondered, if even the servants had been banking on the Viscount making
an advantageous marriage, what would happen in
the future.

It would not be easy to find another girl as rich
as Niobe.

The hackney-carriage reached Berkeley Square

and Jemima paid the driver with some money she had asked the Viscount to give her before she had left the house.

She wondered now whether there would be any more and where he would get it.

She walked into the Hall, taking off her new and very fashionable bonnet as she did so, and thinking she must be careful before she started cooking the luncheon to cover her gown with an apron.

Then as Hawkins came towards her she knew that something was wrong.

"What is it?" she asked.

"There's a gentleman to see you in th' Drawing-Room, M'Lady. Sir Aylmer Barrington!"

Jemima stood very still, as if she was turned to stone.

Her first impulse was to run away, then a pride that had made her defy her uncle in the past came to her rescue and she knew that whatever the consequences, she must face him.

"Where is His Lordship?" she asked Hawkins.

"He'll be back soon, M'Lady. He's gone riding with Mr. Hinlip."

Jemima looked at her reflection in one of the mirrors which hung on the wall, and as she patted her hair into place she was aware that her eyes were large, dark, and frightened.

She could almost feel herself cringe as her uncle had made her do so often just before striking her with his riding-whip, and the constriction in her throat felt familiar and her lips were dry.

Then as if she refused to be a coward she walked resolutely towards the Drawing-Room door and opened it.

Sir Aylmer was standing in front of the mantel-piece, looking overwhelming as he invariably managed to do in Jemima's eyes, even when he was not exerting himself.

She knew by the expression on his face and the tightness of his lips that he was exceedingly incensed.

She felt her heart begin to thump unpleasantly and there was that little tremor in her breast that she recognised as one of fear.

"So here you are, Jemima," Sir Aylmer said in the sharp voice which he always used to his niece, but which would have been a surprise to many of his acquaintances.

"Yes . . . Uncle Aylmer," Jemima said, walking a little way towards him.

"I suppose you think you have been very clever," he said, "marrying—if you are married—a man who is deeply in love with Niobe. But let me tell you, I do not intend to be made a fool of in this manner, and as your marriage is not legal, you are coming back with me. Then I will punish you for your extremely reprehensible behaviour so that you will certainly not run away from me again!"

Sir Aylmer did not raise his voice, which made his words seem all the more intimidating.

"I am . . . sorry . . . Uncle Aylmer, if I have . . . annoyed you," Jemima said, "but you have told me often . . . enough what an . . . encumbrance I am . . . so I cannot . . . believe that you have . . . missed me."

"It is not a question of missing you," Sir Aylmer replied. "It is simply that I will not be defied, nor will I have any niece of mine behaving like a strumpet and going off with the first man who comes her way. Go and fetch your belongings, unless you want me to whip you here and now, as you richly deserve!"

"I think . . . Uncle Aylmer, we should . . . wait to hear what my . . . husband has to say about . . . it."

Jemima's reply seemed to infuriate Sir Alymer to the point where he lost control of himself, and his biting voice changed to a shout as he roared at her:

"You will do as you are told!"

As he spoke he raised his arm and walked towards Jemima as if he would strike her.

As she cringed away from him, unable to prevent herself from showing her terror at what he meant to do, the door opened and the Viscount came into the room.

Sir Aylmer dropped his arm and Jemima without thinking ran towards her husband.

She flung herself against the Viscount, wishing instinctively to hold on to him, but she managed to have enough self-control at the last minute to prevent herself from doing so. Instead she just stood close to him, and he knew she was trembling.

"May I enquire, Sir Aylmer," the Viscount asked in a voice that was extremely sarcastic, "why you are shouting at my wife?"

"Your wife!" Sir Aylmer replied scornfully. "Do you really believe she is your wife? You are not a fool, Ockley—you know as well as I do that in this country no marriage to a girl who is under-age is legal without the permission of her Guardian."

"We were married by Special Licence," the Viscount said, "and the Vicar who performed the ceremony asked me no questions. So I am, if you wish to prefer charges, prepared to answer in front of the Magistrates, and my plea for such precipitate action will be, of course, one of compassion."

"Compassion?" Sir Aylmer questioned.

He did not wait for an answer but said, his voice rising:

"You may bluster and try to excuse your behaviour, Ockley, but I intend to take my niece home with me immediately and give her the thrashing she deserves for leaving my house and foisting herself upon you."

Sir Aylmer's voice had ended once again in a shout, and he was surprised to see a smile on the Viscount's lips as he replied:

"I do hope you will repeat that statement and in exactly those words for the benefit of the Magistrates. As I have already said, whatever other feelings I might have for your niece, I could hardly allow any girl who is little more than a child to be treated with a brutality and an inhumanity which would bring tears to any Juror's eyes."

There was silence when he finished speaking. Then Sir Aylmer said, and now there was a wary look on his face:

"I do not know what you are saying."

"I am saying," the Viscount said sharply, "that if you decide to go before the Magistrates and ask for our marriage to be annulled because it is illegal, I shall bring my wife into Court and show the public how you have treated her. You have left your mark very clearly on her back, and that, Sir Aylmer, will show the world, especially the Social World in which you wish to shine, exactly the type of brute you are!"

The Viscount's voice seemed to ring out in a very different way from the way Sir Aylmer had stormed and ranted.

There was complete silence. Then Sir Aylmer said:

"Perhaps—perhaps I have been somewhat hasty. Of course, if you are content with this extraordinary marriage, there would be no point in my trying to nullify it."

"No point at all!" the Viscount agreed. "And now I am sure, Sir Aylmer, your horses are waiting."

He opened the door as he spoke.

Sir Aylmer stared incredulously.

"Are you throwing me out of your house, Ockley?"

"Not at all," the Viscount replied. "I am merely making it clear that I prefer you outside my front door rather than inside it. Good-day, Sir Aylmer!"

There was nothing Sir Aylmer could do except walk across the room past the Viscount and proceed down the Hall.

His face was contorted with fury and he was muttering beneath his breath.

He reached the front door and had not even descended the steps before Hawkins shut the door noisily behind him.

In the Drawing-Room, the Viscount listened to him leave, and Jemima gave a little cry.

"How could ... you be so ... wonderful? Thank you ... oh ... thank you!"

As she spoke she put her hands up to her eyes to prevent herself from bursting into tears.

Chapter Four

As the Viscount and Jemima drove back to Berkeley Square from where they had been having luncheon, they were laughing.

The news that the Viscount had married a Barrington but not what the Social World called "the right one" had now reached the ears of a number of his friends and acquaintances.

When they set out for luncheon with the Countess of Lincoln, Jemima was sure that the invitation had been sent to them out of sheer curiosity.

This was confirmed when she saw the expressions in the eyes of the guests.

They had arrived a little later than most of the other people who had been invited, and there had been that sudden silence when they were announced which showed that they were being talked about.

Then every eye in the room seemed to watch them speculatively as their hostess greeted them, then took Jemima round to introduce her first to the ladies, then to the gentlemen.

She was conscious, and it gave her confidence, that the gown of leaf-green she was wearing and a bonnet trimmed with ribbons of the same colour were very becoming.

It had been extremely expensive, but she felt, as she heard the compliments that were offered her, that it had been worth every penny.

All through luncheon and afterwards Jemima was bombarded with questions as to why no-one had seen her in London previous to her marriage or, more embarrassingly, why the questioner had not met her when they were entertained by her uncle.

She managed with some cleverness to avoid giving a direct answer, but she was quite certain that when she and the Viscount had left, the other guests would talk over what had been said and would decide that there was some mystery about her.

The Viscount, however, was delighted at the excitement he had caused.

He was well aware as luncheon progressed that Jemima was holding her own with the other ladies, and he knew that the men were fascinated by her looks, which were a complete contrast to the beauty of her cousin.

The Viscount thought with satisfaction that there were at least four people in the room who were intimate friends of Sir Aylmer and Niobe and he was sure that practically everything that was said would be repeated, before the day ended, to Jemima's relatives.

He was still feeling elated by the manner in which he had vanquished Sir Aylmer so completely that he was quite certain Jemima's uncle would not trouble her again in the future.

His success where Sir Aylmer was concerned had also brought him congratulations from Freddy.

"That was clever of you, Valient," he said. "I cannot think how you were quick enough to know that his social reputation was the one thing he would defend at all costs."

"You forget," the Viscount replied, "he was prepared to consider me as a son-in-law only because I had a title."

The bitterness in his voice made his friend aware that the wound to his self-esteem was still very painful, and tactfully he changed the subject, merely adding:

"I am only sorry we cannot tell our friends how cleverly you handled the swine, but it would not do Jemima any good if people were aware that he had beaten her in such a brutal manner."

"No, of course not!" the Viscount agreed. "That must remain a secret between us three."

He thought at the luncheon-party, seeing how smart and elegant Jemima looked, that no-one would credit for a second that she was the same miserable, frightened girl who had hidden under a rug in his Phaeton to escape another beating.

Driving back behind Freddy's horses, which he had lent them so that they could arrive in style, the Viscount had said as soon as they were away from the house:

"That was excellent! We shall have left everybody talking their heads off and that was just what I intended."

"Why does it please you so much?" Jemima enquired.

"Because Niobe will hear of it and of your appearance, and the compliments you were paid will lose nothing in the telling."

"Do you really hate her?"

"You can hardly expect me to have any other feeling."

Jemima could not help thinking first that if one really loved someone, one could not wish to hurt her, and secondly that it would have been impossible, however much the Viscount protested otherwise, to fall out of love so precipitately.

She reasoned it out that while his feelings had been wounded, his pride humiliated, and his ideals shattered, it would be impossible for him to lose his love for Niobe completely.

He had been so ardent in his wooing, and because Niobe liked to show off, Jemima had been given a great number of his letters to read—letters so passionately adoring that they had seemed, Jemima thought, almost to burn the paper on which they were written.

She was very ignorant about love, but at the same time she was sure that it was stronger than human frailty.

She had read about women who had gone on loving their husbands after they became criminals, of Russian aristocrats who had followed their husbands to Siberia because they loved them, of Frenchwomen who had braved the guillotine with a smile on their lips because they could die beside the man to whom they had given their heart.

'That is love,' Jemima thought to herself, 'and

however Niobe behaves, however cruel she may be to him, he will still fundamentally love her because he cannot help it.'

She could at the same time understand the bitterness in his voice, the hardness in his eyes, and the way he was trying to take his revenge by taunting her with his wife.

Sometimes at night she would wake up and wonder what would have happened to her if she had, as she intended, reached London without a friend and with only two guineas between her and starvation.

That she was married to a man who treated her kindly and with consideration, that she was legally entitled to use his name and his title, was such an inexpressible joy that even after being married for several days she still questioned if she was not dreaming.

But more than these things was that she had found what fun it was to be with two men who could laugh with her and listen to her views, and not be beaten for something she had done wrong.

"I am so lucky ... so very ... very lucky. Thank You ... God ... thank You," she said a thousand times a day.

She was sure too that it was her mother who had sent the Viscount to rescue her at exactly the right moment.

When she had been living with her uncle she had sometimes thought that there was no God, no Heaven, and that her father and mother were really dead, so that she could never reach them. But now she knew she had been mistaken.

They were looking after her as they had when

they were alive, and she never need really have been afraid of losing touch with them.

"Well, that is one hurdle over," the Viscount remarked as they drove into Berkeley Square. "I wonder what the next will be."

Jemima was just about to make some light and amusing reply when she saw, to her surprise, Hawkins running down the Square towards them.

"There is Hawkins!" she exclaimed.

The Viscount, having seen his valet at the same time, drew his horses to a standstill.

Hawkins reached the side of the Phaeton and because he had run so quickly he took a second or two to get his breath.

"What is the matter? What has happened?" the Viscount enquired.

"That's what I've come running to tell Your Lordship," Hawkins replied. "There's trouble!"

"What sort of trouble?"

"The tradesmen have found out that Her Ladyship isn't the Miss Barrington they expected."

Jemima gave a little sound as the Viscount asked:

"How do you know this?"

"They're waiting for you, M'Lord—about ten of them—in a nasty mood they be!"

There was silence for a moment. Then the Viscount said:

"Well, there is nothing I can do but face them."

"That's what I thought you'd say, M'Lord, but I thinks I ought to warn you."

"Thank you, Hawkins. You go ahead of us. We will follow slowly."

Hawkins did not argue. He only turned and

started to walk back at a brisk pace towards the house.

The Viscount waited for him to get well ahead before he moved his horses.

"Have you any money with which to pay them?" Jemima asked in a low voice as he did not speak.

"Not a penny!"

"What do you mean—not a penny?" she enquired.

"I am telling you the truth. I have been living on what I could overdraw at the Bank, but they wrote to me yesterday saying they would honour no more cheques."

"But why have you . . ." Jemima began.

Then she bit back the words as they came to her lips.

It was not for her to tell him he had been extremely foolish in running up debts he could not pay.

She thought despairingly that she had just contributed to his financial problems by accepting the expensive gowns that he and Freddy had chosen for her in Bond Street, and also spending a lot on the accessories that she had thought at the time were necessities.

"What will you do?" she asked in a frightened voice.

The Viscount drew up his horses outside his house and Freddy Hinlip's groom was waiting ready to take the reins from him.

The Viscount did not reply.

He stepped down from the Phaeton and had already taken two steps when he remembered his manners and went back to assist Jemima to alight.

They walked side by side through the front door, which Hawkins opened for them, to find that the men he had warned them about were waiting in the Hall.

They were all tradesmen. One Jemima was sure was a butcher, another she suspected of being a wine-merchant, while the man who stepped towards them and had obviously been chosen as their spokesman was, she felt from the smartness of his clothes, a tailor.

She was not mistaken.

"Good-afternoon, Gentlemen!" the Viscount said in a quite genial tone. "What can I do for you?"

"I think Your Lordship knows the answer to that," the spokesman replied. "I represent Mr. Weston, M'Lord, and I have here a bill for three hundred eighty-five pounds which is much overdue, and we must request payment immediately!"

The other men in the Hall also produced bills, waving them at the Viscount as if they were flags, and shouting as they did so:

"My bill's for one hundred eighty pounds!" "Mine's two hundred!" "Mine's ninety-five!"

It was difficult to distinguish what was said in the general uproar, but it was quite obvious that they were aggressive, and their voices were harsh and demanding.

"Perhaps you would care to tell me," the Viscount said coldly and speaking with almost a drawl, "why you have suddenly decided to confront me at this particular moment in such an unseemly fashion."

"Your Lordship knows the answer to that too," the man who came from Weston's replied.

"I have no idea. So perhaps you would explain in plain English."

Listening, Jemima knew that the men, being somewhat in awe of a nobleman, were feeling uncomfortable.

Then a man at the back who could barely be seen shouted:

"Ye didn't marry the bride us expected!"

"How very remiss of me!" the Viscount said sarcastically. "But I hardly imagine all clients consult you before they enter into the bonds of matrimony!"

"Fine words won't pay our bills, M'Lord," the tailor said, "and we're all in agreement."

"About what?"

"That if you won't pay, we'll seize what you possess, or if you prefers we'll put it under the hammer."

There was a little pause after he had spoken. Then the Viscount replied, still in the sarcastic voice he had used before:

"If you do that, you will come up against the Law. I own nothing in my own right. The Estate, my houses, the furniture, the paintings—all are entailed on my heirs."

There was silence after he had spoken and Jemima could see that they were discomfited by the news and uncertain as to what they should do.

Then the man who had spoken before shouted:

"Then 'tis th' Fleet for ye, M'Lord! An' there ye'll stay 'til ye pays us!"

Jemima gave a little gasp.

She knew that the Fleet Prison for Debtors was filled with men who languished there, by order of the Court, in appalling conditions until their relatives or friends could bail them out by paying their debts.

She looked at the Viscount in horror and saw that with admirable self-control his expression had not changed.

However, she knew that he was perturbed, because as she stood beside him she could see a little pulse beating in his temple.

"If that is your attitude," he said after a moment's pause, "then there is nothing I can do about it. But, however hard you may try, you cannot get blood out of a stone!"

There was a sound from the assembled men almost, Jemima thought, like that made by fox-hounds when they pull down their prey.

Then before anyone could speak she said:

"I wish to say something."

Because it was so unexpected, not only the creditors but also the Viscount himself turned to look at her in surprise.

She knew that they were listening, and although her heart was beating tumultuously and it was difficult to breathe, she managed to say slowly and in a clear voice:

"I may not be the Barrington you expected His Lordship to marry, but I am Sir Aylmer's niece and I think I may have a solution to this problem."

As if he appreciated that she was making an effort on their behalf, the tailor said:

"We'd be glad to hear it, M'Lady."

"As His Lordship has just told you," Jemima went on, "he cannot sell a house that is entailed, but there is no reason why this house should not command a good rent if it was let."

She saw the expression on the men's faces and said quickly:

"It may not be much towards what you are owed, but at least it will be something, and now that His Lordship knows how urgent the problem is, I am certain there will be other monies in the future."

After a short silence the same aggressive man who had spoken before said:

" 'Ow d' yer know ye'll find anyone t' rent this 'ere place?"

"Actually I have somebody in mind," Jemima replied, "and what I would like to suggest, gentlemen, is that you give His Lordship twenty-four hours to see if he and I can find some of the money you are owed. I am sure he will promise that the whole rent, without deductions, will be divided proportionally between you."

She saw the uncertainty in their eyes and added:

"This, you will agree, is a gesture towards settling your accounts, and you have a choice: if you send His Lordship to the Fleet you will get nothing, but if you leave him free, he and I together will do what we can to pay off his debts completely in the shortest possible time."

For a moment Jemima thought despairingly that she had failed and they would not accept her offer.

Then the tailor who was standing nearest to her, perhaps moved by the sincerity in her voice and the undoubted attractiveness of her appearance, said:

"Would Your Ladyship let me discuss what you've just suggested with my colleagues? We'll not keep you and His Lordship waiting for long."

Jemima looked at the Viscount and he said hastily:

"We will wait in the Drawing-Room."

He walked forward and the men parted to allow him and Jemima to move through them.

Hawkins opened the door and they walked in and heard it close behind them.

The Viscount did not speak but walked to the end of the room to stand at the mantelpiece looking down into the empty fireplace.

"I am . . . sorry if what I said was . . . impertinent," Jemima said in a very small voice, "but I was . . . afraid . . . terribly afraid, that they would . . . send you to the . . . Fleet."

"It was quick-witted of you to do what you did," the Viscount replied. "What I am asking myself is how I could have allowed things to go on for so long without realising what was the inevitable end of a Rake's progress."

"Perhaps you can . . . manage to pay them . . . back as I . . . suggested."

"How?" he enquired. "Do you really think you can find a tenant for this place?"

"I think I know somebody who would take it," Jemima said, "but of course it is not going to be enough to pay all those bills."

"Even if you are clever enough to rid me of my London home, I am quite certain nobody would give me two pence for Ockley Priory!"

"Perhaps there is some other way you could find to make money there?"

The Viscount laughed and it was a rather unpleasant, jeering sound.

"If there were, my father would have exploited it

years ago! No, Jemima, you had better let me go to the Fleet and have done with it!"

"How can you be so chicken-hearted?" she retorted without thinking. "The one thing I never expected you to be was a coward!"

"A coward?"

The Viscount turned and there was no doubt that he was angry.

"I have been accused of many things in my time," he said, "but no-one has ever suggested that I am a coward."

"Then you had better start fighting," Jemima flashed at him, "because this is your Waterloo!"

He stared at her furiously for some seconds, then suddenly he began to laugh.

It was so unexpected that she stared back at him, and after a moment as he went on laughing she asked:

"What do you . . . find so . . . funny?"

"You!" he said. "You look like a bantam fighting-cock attacking me, and it suddenly struck me as amusing that I should be nagged into battle by a woman when I have always thought in the past that if anything I have lived too dangerously."

"You may not be risking your life in this battle," Jemima replied, "but if you lose your freedom it will hardly be worth living anyway."

The Viscount laughed again. Then he said in a more serious tone:

"You are right, Jemima, of course you are right! And if you really know of some Midas who would offer a fortune for this house I shall be grateful. I only hope he exists, otherwise the gentlemen out-

side are going to make themselves extremely unpleasant."

"He really exists," Jemima replied, "and we will
go and see him as soon as our visitors have left."

"They may refuse to leave, except to take me before the Magistrates."

"Stop being so faint-hearted," Jemima replied,
and the Viscount laughed again.

As he did so, the door opened and Hawkins
said:

"They'd like to speak to you, M'Lord."

The Viscount walked towards the door. He did
not invite Jemima to come with him, but she had
no intention of being left behind.

Once again it was obvious that the tailor was to
be their spokesman.

"Have you come to any decision?" the Viscount
enquired.

"We have decided, M'Lord," the tailor replied,
"to give Her Ladyship's suggestion a chance, but
we wishes to make it clear that we receives the
whole rent for this house, and we also expects,
M'Lord, quite substantial sums from other sources
to reach us before Christmas."

"I accept your proposition," the Viscount said,
"and as soon as arrangements have been made to
let the house, I will ensure that the monies I receive in rent are handed over to you to be divided
as Her Ladyship suggested."

"Thank you, M'Lord. Thank you."

Now that they had extracted at least an offer,
the manner in which they spoke became very different, and watching them Jemima was sure that

some of them felt embarrassed and even a little apprehensive about the way they had behaved.

She thought miserably that it was all her fault.

They might never have been driven into open confrontation if the Viscount had not flaunted his loss of an heiress by marrying someone else.

She was quite certain that the tradesmen, if no-one else, knew that she was a poor relation.

They were always closely in league with the servants in big houses; it only needed one skivy in Sir Aylmer's household in London to tell anyone who enquired how insignificant and unimportant Jemima was, and the information would run like wildfire through the rest of the Viscount's creditors.

'I must help him, I must!' she thought desperately.

As if the Viscount thought the same thing, when Hawkins closed the front door, he asked:

"Well, what do we do now?"

"We go to the City in a hired hackney-carriage," Jemima replied.

"To the City?" the Viscount repeated in surprise.

But Hawkins, without being instructed, was already running into the Square, whistling through his fingers to a hackney-carriage waiting under the trees.

*　*　*

Driving towards the City at a very much slower rate and by no means as elegantly as they had travelled in Freddy's Phaeton, Jemima told the Viscount what they were going to do.

"Although I was never allowed to have luncheon

with Uncle Aylmer when he had several guests, sometimes when he entertained his business associates he told me to be present as a substitute for Niobe."

She saw that the Viscount did not understand, and she explained:

"Niobe would have behaved in a grand and condescending manner to them, and Uncle Aylmer was shrewd enough to realise they would resent it. But when they were invited to the house they naturally expected to meet his family, and I was therefore ordered to make myself pleasant."

"And did you?" the Viscount asked with a smile.

"Some of them were really rather nice," Jemima replied. "Besides, it was fascinating to see how different they were from the aristocrats like yourself."

She saw that the Viscount was listening and she went on:

"They were hard, shrewd, calculating, and sometimes a little uncouth, but they all had one thing in common."

"What was that?"

"An aura of success. Perhaps it was a driving ambition, perhaps a power they had evolved because they were determined to have their own way, but a vibration came from them which I found intensely interesting."

She paused and the Viscount said:

"Go on! I understand what you are telling me."

"Mr. Joshua Roseburg, whom we are calling on now, was typical of them, except that he was even more successful than most of them."

"What does he do?"

"I think he has been involved in almost anything that can make money," Jemima replied. "I know that years ago Uncle Aylmer and he were partners in the slave-trade."

"In slavery?" the Viscount exclaimed with a frown.

"Despicable though it was," Jemima said, "there is no doubt that a great many people in England made a lot of money out of it."

"That is what I have always heard."

"Then, as soon as it began to be discredited," Jemima went on, "Uncle Aylmer was no longer interested, but I think both he and Mr. Roseburg had by that time made a fortune."

"Why did your uncle continue the association?"

"He of course did not talk at meal-times in front of me," Jemima said, "but I picked up little references from here and there and I became aware that Mr. Roseburg is useful to Uncle Aylmer and he is a person my uncle has no wish to offend."

"What makes you think he would be interested in renting my house?"

"Once when we had had luncheon at Uncle Aylmer's house in London he said as he was leaving:

" 'Well, I must go back to work, Sir Aylmer. You're lucky you can enjoy yourself in a place like this.'

"He looked round the Drawing-Room as he spoke and I knew that he was envious of the paintings and the furniture.

" 'There is nothing to stop you from buying a house as good as this, if not better,' Uncle Aylmer answered.

"Mr. Roseburg gave a short laugh.

" 'What chance do I have of rubbing shoulders with the Big Nobs like you?' he asked. 'If I had any such pretentions, I would doubtless be told to get back to Cheapside, where I belong!' "

"And what makes you think he will rent my house?" the Viscount asked sharply.

"When he had left, Uncle Aylmer said to me: 'And quite right! We cannot have people like Roseburg setting themselves up as gentlemen!' "

Jemima's voice dropped as she added:

"He then struck me because I had annoyed him by something I had said, and as it was very painful I forgot about Mr. Roseburg. But I am sure that if he had the chance, he would wish to rent a house like yours in the very heart of Mayfair."

She knew without the Viscount speaking that he was sceptical and thought her over-optimistic.

When they reached Mr. Roseburg's office in Cheapside and were shown into his private sanctum, the Viscount was surprised at the effusive way in which he greeted them.

"Well, well, Your Ladyship, this is indeed an honour!" he said to Jemima. "When I was told it was you and not your cousin who had married His Lordship, I called my informant a liar!"

"No, Mr. Roseburg, it is quite true," Jemima said, "and let me introduce my husband, who is very anxious to meet you."

Mr. Roseburg held out his hand.

At the same time, after he had invited them to sit down and ordered a servant to give them a glass of wine, Jemima was aware, as was the Viscount, that he eyed them a little warily.

"Now what can I do for you young people?" he enquired.

There was no doubt that there was now a businesslike note in his voice which intimated that he thought they had come to borrow money.

Jemima smiled at him.

"I think, Mr. Roseburg," she said, "we can offer you a chance to realise one of your ambitions. At the same time, you can help us."

"How can I do that?"

"His Lordship and I are anxious to retire to the country," Jemima said, "and it would be nice to honeymoon there away from all our friends, who have most kindly overwhelmed us with invitations when, as you can well understand, we would prefer to be alone."

She gave the Viscount a glance which she hoped was both shy and affectionate and would deceive Mr. Roseburg into thinking they were very much in love.

"Then what's the difficulty, Your Ladyship?" Mr. Roseburg enquired.

"His Lordship's house in Berkeley Square needs someone to look after it, Mr. Roseburg, and we thought that you might like to be our tenant."

The expression on Mr. Roseburg's face told her that the idea had never entered his mind.

"I have heard you admire Uncle Aylmer's London house," Jemima went on, "but His Lordship's is older and, to my mind, more attractive, and we have some very distinguished neighbours. What is more, I am sure that Mrs. Roseburg and your family would find it comfortable and very convenient for the shops and the Theatres."

As she was talking she was aware that Mr. Roseburg was assimilating the idea.

She was sure that his sharp, agile mind was already taking in the advantages of being the tenant of a nobleman and living in a house to which he would be proud to invite his business-colleagues.

"It is an idea I haven't entertained before, My Lady," he said when Jemima paused for breath. "How much were you thinking of asking?"

"As much as you will give us!" Jemima said disarmingly. "As you are well aware, Mr. Roseburg, and I will be very frank with you, I am not an heiress like my cousin, and my husband has found life very expensive since he left his Regiment."

Mr. Roseburg laughed.

"You were always one to speak your mind," he said, "which is one of the reasons why I looked forward to seeing you when I called on your uncle. I used to think to myself it was a pity you were not a boy; we might have done business together."

"That is what I am asking you to do now, Mr. Roseburg!"

"So you are! So you are!" he said with some surprise. "What does His Lordship think about this?"

He looked at the Viscount as he spoke.

"From all my wife has told me about you, Mr. Roseburg," the Viscount said, "I should be both delighted and honoured for you to occupy my house."

"Well, you can't say fairer than that!" Mr. Roseburg remarked.

"Why do you not come and see it this afternoon when you have finished in the City?" Jemima enquired. "And of course bring Mrs. Roseburg if she is free."

"The Missus leaves such decisions to me," Mr. Roseburg said. "But I accept your invitation, M'Lady, and I'll be with you at five o'clock, if that suits His Lordship?"

"I shall look forward to seeing you, Mr. Roseburg," the Viscount replied.

* * *

Driving back in the hackney-carriage, Jemima said:

"He will take it, but I am wondering what we ought to ask."

"Anything we can get," the Viscount replied. "I suppose you know what you are letting yourself in for?"

"Tell me?" Jemima replied.

"You will find the Priory damned uncomfortable."

"Why?"

"Because it was left to go to rack and ruin during the war when I was away in France and my father was living in London. There was no money to do any repairs while first my father and then I stayed on in London. I never went back except to see that there was more and more dilapidation each time I visited it."

"I suppose there will be a roof over our heads?"

"I hope so, although undoubtedly it has holes in it."

"Who has been looking after it?"

"Nobody. I could not afford to pay any servants,

and those who have been pensioned off were simply asked to keep an eye on it."

"But there are furniture and beds, and I presume pots and pans with which to cook?"

"I cannot answer that question fully, as I do not really know," the Viscount replied. "But yes, there is furniture in the rooms, and paintings on the walls, but the rest may have been eaten by mice, or stolen."

There was silence. Then Jemima said in a low voice:

"But there is no alternative . . . is there?"

"None, unless we batten on our friends. As it happens, Freddy's house is not far away."

"No!" Jemima said sharply.

"Why do you say it like that?"

"Because as a poor relation let me tell you there is nothing worse than feeling beholden to people and getting further and further into debt. I have a feeling, although you may think I am wrong, that you should start again from scratch and stand on your own feet."

She felt the Viscount stiffen beside her before he said:

"You certainly have a very accurate way, Jemima, of hitting below the belt."

"Hawkins is very fond of you," she said, "that is obvious. But I am sure that morally things are very different now that you have a wife."

"I follow your reasoning," the Viscount said, "although I must say that in entering the happy state of matrimony it did not strike me that I should have to take on other burdens besides the obvious ones."

"Well, you have!" Jemima said simply. "And I

think this is a battle we have to fight ourselves,
without relying on other people permanently coming to our rescue, even if they should offer to do
so."

"I have a feeling you are not only pointing me
in the right direction," the Viscount said, "but
warning me about what I should not do."

"I think you know it yourself, and I am only ex-
pressing what is in my own mind for my own satisfaction."

"Pretty words, but unpleasant facts!" the Viscount remarked.

As she looked at him Jemima was not certain
whether or not he was annoyed with her.

* * *

Three days later Jemima had her first glimpse of
Ockley Priory, which had lost its status during the
Dissolution of the Monasteries during the reign of
Henry VIII and had been acquired two centuries
later by an Ockley who thought it an attractive
building.

It had been added on to by succeeding generations but its intrinsic beauty had remained un-
changed, and as Jemima saw it she gave a little
exclamation of delight.

"It is lovely!" she exclaimed. "Really lovely!"

It certainly looked so in the distance, set beside a
stream where the monks had once fished for trout
and sheltered by a thick fir wood.

It was built of soft grey stone and its twisting
chimneys were silhouetted against the sky.

It might, with its many-paned windows, have
typified a monk's desire for a quiet, cloistered life,

and Jemima felt somehow as if there was something familiar about it and in some strange and extraordinary manner she was coming home.

"Wait until you see what it is like inside," the Viscount said drily as they drove on, having once again borrowed Freddy's Phaeton to get them from London to the country.

Freddy had offered the Viscount his Phaeton and horses, and although Jemima knew they should have refused, she also knew it would be very expensive to hire a vehicle to take them there and it was better on this occasion to swallow their pride and just be grateful.

Freddy was delighted that they would be near his home, which was only eight miles away, although he could hardly believe that they intended to live in the country forever.

It was Jemima who had taken him on one side to explain the reason.

"Has Valient told you," she asked, "why we are forced to leave London?"

"He did say something about having a good offer for his house in Berkeley Square."

"His creditors threatened him with the Fleet!"

"Good God!"

There was no doubt that Freddy was astonished.

"I had no idea it was as bad as that," he went on, "although of course I was aware that Valient was a bit 'below hatches.'"

Before Jemima could speak he added:

"You know as well as I do that I would have got him out of the Fleet."

"I was sure you would feel like that," Jemima answered, "but His Lordship has to face facts, and the fact is that he has no money and has to do something about it."

"In what way?"

"We do not yet know. We have found a tenant for the house in Berkeley Square, and when we get to the Priory I have to think of some way of making and saving money so that we can live."

Freddy looked at her, then said:

"You will think this is a strange thing to say, Jemima, but you are exactly the sort of woman Valient has needed in his life for a long time."

"In what way?" Jemima asked.

"Someone who would make him exert himself not at sport but in living."

He paused for a moment before he said:

"I cannot tell you how magnificent Valient was in the war. He not only was exceedingly brave, but he looked after his men and he had a power of leadership which I know quite frankly I have never had myself."

"But the war is over now," Jemima said simply.

"Exactly!" Freddy agreed. "I think that Valient has been drifting about ever since, trying to find a way in which to exercise his mind and his ability. Now perhaps you will find it for him."

"No, no!" Jemima said quickly. "That is the whole point! He has to find it for himself. It is what he must do that is important—not what we for for him!"

Freddy looked at her for a long time. Then he said:

"You tell me what you want me to do, and I will do it."

Jemima smiled at him.

"That is what I hoped you would say, so please do not be too generous until he has had a look round. I am rather apprehensive myself as to what we shall find at Ockley Priory."

"Rats, ruin, and rust!" Freddy answered.

Jemima laughed a little ruefully.

Now, driving down the unkept drive, she could understand why marriage to an heiress had been of so much importance.

Of course Valient had wanted a wife who could restore the ancestral home and make it possible for him to live there.

That he had fallen in love with Niobe because she was so beautiful was an unexpected bonus. At the same time, he had not disguised the fact that her money was vitally important.

Jemima gave a little sigh.

'Why could I not have been rich too?' she wondered.

Then she knew that while there was no happiness in Sir Aylmer's house, her home had been a place of sunshine and laughter.

'We cannot have everything in life!' she thought to herself firmly, 'and we must make the best of what we have.'

That, she knew, was to make the best of a house that needed money spent on it, contriving somehow, without that most necessary commodity, to live as comfortably as possible.

As the Viscount drew his horses up in front of the Priory door she saw the expression on his face, and she said:

"This is where we start our great adventure."

He looked at her as if for explanation, and she said:

"You must realise it is very exciting. We are exploring an unknown land and somehow we have to survive. If that is not the beginning of an adventure, I would like to know what is!"

There was a lilt in her voice and a light in her eyes which for the moment seemed to sweep away the Viscount's depression.

"I hope your optimism will be justified, Jemima," he said in a somewhat sober tone.

"If it is not," Jemima teased, "we can always drown ourselves in the lake. It is not such a bad death when it is so hot, but I have the feeling that, for the moment at any rate, we may have to wash in it."

The darkness vanished from the Viscount's face and he laughed.

"I think that is one prediction that may well come true," he said. "But let us go and explore, and be careful the cobwebs do not strangle you."

He jumped down from the Phaeton and helped Jemima to alight.

Hawkins, who had been riding in the small seat behind, climbed into the Viscount's place.

"I'll take it round to the stables, M'Lord," he said, "and hope to find someone as will help me with the trunks."

"I doubt it," the Viscount answered, "but I will give you a hand myself later."

"That is the spirit!" Jemima said as they stood in front of the huge nail-studded oak door with its iron hinges.

The Viscount drew the key from his pocket.

"Are you ready?" he asked. "When you see what is inside, you will be in for an unpleasant surprise!"

"I like surprises!" Jemima said firmly. "Has our life together so far been anything else?"

"No, that is true," the Viscount agreed, "so here goes!"

He turned the key in the lock and Jemima held her breath.

Chapter Five

Jemima was scrubbing the kitchen-table when she heard footsteps coming down the flagged passage. They stopped at the door.

"Did you have any luck?" she asked without turning round.

"Only in finding you being a good House-keeper!" answered a voice she had not expected.

She gave a little cry and turned round to see Freddy looking exceedingly elegant, almost, she thought, opulent.

She was conscious that she looked the exact opposite.

Under a large and now rather dirty apron she was wearing the gown in which she had run away from her uncle's house.

She would not dare, while she was doing house-work, to wear any of the beautiful and expensive gowns, still unpaid for, which had come from Bond Street, and she had not expected visitors.

She was aware that not only were her hands red

from the amount of scrubbing she had done in the last few days, but also her hair was curling untidily round her forehead from the exertion she had been putting into cleaning the table.

"You should ring the bell before you walk into other people's houses," she said with mock severity.

"I did," Freddy replied, "but I am quite certain it is broken."

Jemima laughed.

"You are right. It is another case of rats, ruin, and rust!"

Freddy walked farther into the kitchen and turned a hard wooden chair round to sit astride it, his arms on the back.

"I rather expected to find you doing this sort of thing. But can you not find a servant in the village?"

"We cannot afford servants," Jemima answered, "although, as a matter of fact, the pensioners have been absolutely marvellous!"

As she spoke, she put her scrubbing-brush into the pail of water and set it to one side. Then she took off her apron, hoping she looked a little better without it.

"You told me to stay away, and I have done so," Freddy said, "until my curiosity could be contained no longer. Tell me what has been happening."

"Exactly what we expected," Jemima replied. "When we arrived, the place was so thick with cobwebs and dust that it was difficult to breathe."

"So you cleaned it up."

"With the help of Hawkins and, believe it or not, Valient."

"He really helped you?" Freddy asked in surprise.

Jemima smiled.

"Actually I find he is far more useful out-of-doors than in. So Hawkins, I, and the pensioners have now made some of the rooms habitable."

"I thought perhaps you would like to put me up."

"No!"

"That is very inhospitable of you!"

"You would be most uncomfortable."

"I was a great deal more uncomfortable in the war."

"That was different. Because you have been so kind to Valient, I would feel embarrassed if you had to wash in cold water and sleep in torn sheets."

"If those are your only objections, I am staying here and there is nothing you can do about it."

"Very well," Jemima answered in the tone of one giving in to the inevitable, "but do not complain if the mice run over your bed when you are asleep and you find that they have nibbled your expensive clothes."

"You are trying to frighten me," Freddy said accusingly. "I have missed you, Jemima, and quite frankly London has been very dull without Valient."

Jemima gave a little cry.

"Please, please do not tell him so! He has for the moment resigned himself to being here, and because he finds he has so much to do, he has not missed London as much as I was afraid he would."

"It is his own fault that he got into such a state of penury," Freddy said. "Why did he not tell me that things were so bad? I keep thinking of the extravagances we committed which were quite unnecessary."

"It is no use regretting," Jemima answered. "What is done is done! Valient has to learn to live within his means, and although I am not quite certain how we can do so, we both have to try."

She paused before she said in a different tone:

"It was very kind of you to give him the money which we are spending now, but I did ask you not to."

"I did not give it to him," Freddy retorted, "I bought his gold watch from him."

"With the proviso that you would return it whenever he could afford to pay you back the money!" Jemima said. "How can I make Valient understand that he cannot expect his friends to bail him out of every scrape, if you aid and abet him?"

There was a cry of despair in Jemima's voice which Freddy did not miss.

While she had been talking, his eyes had been on her face and he wondered how many other women would have been so natural and unselfconscious if they had been discovered doing an ignominious task which should have been done by a servant.

"One exciting thing has happened which Valient will tell you about himself," Jemima said, as if she was determined to sound cheerful.

"What is that?" Freddy enquired.

"One of our tenant-farmers had two unbroken horses which Valient has said he will train. So at least we shall have something to ride."

"I was going to suggest that I send over two of

my own horses for that very purpose, but I wanted first to see what the stables were like."

"No, Freddy," Jemima said pleadingly, "and I am not only thinking of Valient but of you. The farmer's horses are good enough for us."

"Suppose the animal throws you and you are smashed up? What good will that do?"

"As it happens, I am a very good rider, and because my father was poor I have never ridden the sort of horse-flesh you own."

"That is why I would like to offer them to you now."

"But you will refrain from doing so, because I have asked you not to."

"I suppose so," Freddy said ruefully, "and I realise what you are trying to do, Jemima, and I admire you for it. I did not know that a woman could be so magnificent in such adverse conditions."

His words made Jemima shy and she gave him a little half-smile and would have turned away from the table if he had not said:

"Why in God's name could I not have picked you up when you ran away from your uncle's house?"

"Valient did not pick me up—I forced myself upon him!"

"I would have been delighted for you to force yourself upon me."

There was something in Freddy's voice which made Jemima look at him in surprise. Then he said:

"Will it bore you, Jemima, if I tell you the

reason why I could stay away no longer was that I wanted to see you?"

Jemima's eyes dropped before his and he went on:

"I think I fell in love with you when I first saw you looking untidy and frightened and at the same time so absurdly lovely, and already Valient's wife."

"Please . . . Freddy, you must not . . . talk to me like this . . . you know you . . . must not say such things . . . I cannot listen."

"Why not? It is not as though I am trying to seduce you away from a man who wants you for himself."

He saw by the flicker of Jemima's eye-lashes and the little sigh that escaped her lips that his words hurt her. Then she said:

"Valient has been kind to me. He saved me when I was desperate enough to run away to London alone . . . and I shall . . . always be . . . grateful to him."

"You may be grateful," Freddy said, "but is he sufficiently grateful to you for what you are doing for him?"

"What I am doing?" Jemima questioned with a little helpless gesture of her hands. "Do you not realise that if he had not married me in that impetuous manner in order to avenge himself on Niobe, he could, I am sure, have easily found another heiress, while I am just an added encumbrance."

There was silence. Then Freddy said in a very different tone:

"Supposing I took Valient's encumbrance off

his hands? If I asked you, would you come away with me, Jemima?"

His words startled her and she looked at him wide-eyed before she said:

"Are you being serious?"

"Of course I am serious," he answered. "I love you, I want you, and I swear I would make you a great deal happier than Valient is able to do. You certainly would not have to scrub floors or live in this sort of squalor."

Jemima was still for a moment, then she said:

"I shall always be proud to think that you asked me to come with you, but you know the answer without my saying it."

"But why? Why will you not do as I ask?"

"The real reason, apart from any convention or question of right and wrong, is that I do not love you."

"I will teach you to love me."

Jemima shook her head.

"Love is not like that. It is either there or it is not, and nothing one can say or do can alter it."

There was something in her voice which made Freddy know that they were not only talking about themselves.

"Are you telling me," Freddy said after a moment, "that Valient is still in love with that spoilt, obnoxious cousin of yours?"

"Of course he is. That is why he thinks about her all the time and imagines he is hating her when really he loves her as much as he always ... did."

There was a little sob in Jemima's voice on the last word which Freddy did not miss.

"Now I understand why you are refusing me. You love him!"

Jemima did not answer and he asked insistently:

"You really love him, Jemima?"

She gave a deep sigh.

"Yes, I love him. I have loved him, I think, since first I saw him ages ago when he came to call on Niobe, and then wrote her letters which I would have given up my hope of Heaven to receive myself."

As if he could not bear to listen to what Jemima was saying, Freddy rose from the chair and walked across to the kitchen-window to stare out onto the dirty, untidy yard outside.

"What you are telling me is that I have no chance."

"Of course not," Jemima said. "You could not possibly want to cause a scandal by ... running away with a woman who is already married ... and to your best ... friend! Think what everyone would say! While Valient would laugh, it would damage your reputation ... and because I am so ... very, very fond of you, Freddy ... that is ... something I would ... never do."

"You are mothering me as well as Valient," Freddy said with a wry smile.

Jemima gave a little laugh.

"You are right! That is exactly what I feel like ... a rather anxious mother with two ... unpredictable but very ... adorable sons."

Freddy turned round.

"If you talk like that," he said, "I shall abduct you, whatever you may say! I shall take you away to cover you in jewels and teach you how to be happy, so that I no longer see that droop to your lips and the loneliness in your eyes."

Jemima looked startled.

"Do I really . . . look like . . . that?"

"Only when Valient is being particularly difficult or you are wondering how you can pay for the next meal."

Jemima looked at him a little uncertainly, and as if he was suddenly thinking more of her than himself he said:

"I did not come here to add to your troubles, and to be sure of a welcome I have not only brought you some food that you will not have to cook but also a case of champagne for Valient!"

Before Jemima could speak a voice, from the door exclaimed:

"Did I hear the word 'champagne'?"

"Hello, Valient!" Freddy exclaimed as the Viscount walked into the kitchen.

He threw down on the kitchen-table two ducks and three rabbits, saying in a tone of satisfaction:

"Not bad for a morning's work! At least we can offer you a bite to eat, Freddy."

"I have brought more than a bite with me," Freddy answered, "but I see you have not forgotten how to handle a gun."

"This old blunderbuss is out-of-date," the Viscount replied, looking down at the gun he held under his arm, "and to be honest, I found a Frenchman was a larger target. I have wasted quite a lot of cartridges, which we can ill-afford."

"Never mind—every little bit helps," Jemima said with a smile. "I will hang these up in the game-larder."

The Viscount made no effort to do it for her but sat on the edge of the kitchen-table, saying as he did so:

"I am very glad to see you, Freddy. Why have you not come before?"

"I have been in London, as it happens."

He saw the glint in his friend's eye and added quickly:

"I cannot tell you what a bore it has been, the same old parties every night, the same old gossip. Since you left there has been nothing left to talk about."

"Are they talking about Jemima and me?"

There was silence, as if Freddy considered what he should say. Then he remarked:

"Niobe's engagement to the Marquis was announced this morning!"

"Well, at least I pipped her at the post!" the Viscount remarked.

"I am quite sure she is aware that her engagement is an anticlimax."

"If you have brought some champagne, at least we can drink to her ill-health and her unhappiness!" the Viscount said. "Where have you put it?"

"I have brought a groom with me," Freddy answered, "so I imagine he will carry it into the Hall."

"Then let us go and find it," the Viscount said eagerly. "The only thing left in the cellar here is some wine long past its best, which was why my father did not drink it!"

"I rather imagined that would be the case," Freddy said. "But I intend to stay with you, if you will have me, so I have brought my own rations."

"Quite right!" the Viscount approved.

He led the way towards the front of the house, and as they went down one of the long corridors which Jemima felt still had a peace about them which came from the first holy inhabitants of the Priory, they encountered Freddy's groom.

He was carrying a box filled with food, and before the Viscount could ask the question he explained to his Master:

"I thought I should take this to th' kitchen, Sir, and where would you wish me to put th' wine?"

"You will find the kitchen at the end of this passage," Freddy replied, "and His Lordship and I will deal with the wine."

"Very good, Sir."

It was after they had enjoyed the luncheon, which consisted mostly of the things which Freddy had brought with him, that Jemima, watching the Viscount laugh in a manner in which he had not done since they came to the Priory, told herself she was glad that Freddy had joined them.

At first she had been much worried and almost terrified by the condition of the house, realizing how much they had to do to get it habitable. But she was determined not to let the Viscount know her true feelings.

She laughed at him when he became entangled in the cobwebs and called him faint-hearted when he said it would be an Herculean task for anyone to sweep away the dust of ages!

The first night they had more or less camped in bedrooms that smelt of dust and decay.

It was Hawkins who had found that the pensioners would be only too pleased to help for a few pence a day, and although some of them were so old they did very little, every little bit helped.

Jemima was in fact captivated by the beauty of the Priory itself, with its thick walls and quiet cloisters, and its beautiful Refectory, which had withstood the wear and tear of the years as well as the turbulent ups and downs of history.

It had survived, and Jemima told herself that she and the Viscount could do the same.

For the first few days she was so tired when she went to bed that she knew she would have slept if she had just lain down on the dusty carpet.

Gradually conditions improved and it became a game to see how much she could achieve every day and exciting to see how different the house itself had begun to look.

She knew it was important that the Viscount, and of course Hawkins, should have enough to eat, so it had been a relief to find that they did not have to spend as much money as they would have done had there not been plenty of food available in the Park and in the woods.

It was not the right season for game, but the young rabbits were delicious, and there was duck, and although Jemima did not like to think they must kill them, there were far too many deer.

These had done an enormous amount of destruction in the gardens, which had become almost a jungle, but to the Viscount's surprise he found that the kitchen-gardens were still being cultivated.

This was due to the male pensioners, who, having nothing much to do, had decided it was easier to grow what they needed in the kitchen-gardens, which had once been properly dug and maintained by an army of gardeners.

The old men were only too willing to let Jemima have anything she wished in the way of vegetables, lettuces, and radishes, and they would have been embarrassed if she had insisted on paying.

She had, however, insisted on paying for the eggs and butter from the farmers, since she had the anxious feeling that while they were prepared to be generous they were only waiting for an excuse to ask the Viscount to do repairs which were badly needed on their farm-buildings.

Jemima often found herself thinking how attractive the Priory and the surroundings must have been when the Viscount was a small boy and there had been money to ensure that everything ran perfectly and there were plenty of servants in every department.

"I have never seen so many vermin!" the Viscount said angrily when he came back from the woods. "We need at least six game-keepers, as we used to have in my grandfather's day."

"I would insist first on having six house-maids!" Jemima answered.

"I cannot think why!" he said teasingly. "The house looks almost back to normal, while I want grooms in the stables, gardeners, keepers, and at least a dozen horses on which to ride round the Estate and give my orders."

Jemima had thrown at him the duster she was holding in her hand and he had caught it and thrown it back.

"Stop annoying me!" she said. "And if you have nothing better to do, you might catch a trout for dinner. I am sure you are growing tired of having soup every night."

"Not the way you make it," the Viscount replied. "And that reminds me—I think soon we ought to have a dinner-party."

He had been joking, but Jemima took him seriously.

"If you dare to invite one person inside the Priory before I have it looking decent, I will walk out. You have no idea how much there is still to do."

He had laughed, and when he had gone Jemima thought despairingly that without money and without help, it would be impossible for her ever to get the Priory into even passable working order.

In every room one or two window-panes were cracked or missing, and in some rooms the floorboards had given way, and in others the ceilings had fallen down.

It had been impossible for the first three days for them to have any hot water, and while the Viscount had swum in the lake, Jemima had bathed in cold water and tried to pretend it did not make her shiver.

Now, with Freddy making the Viscount laugh, she felt that every effort had been not only worthwhile but not as difficult as it had seemed at first.

"We are winning!" she told herself. "We are winning!"

Then she asked the question that was always at the back of her mind:

"What of the future?"

From the moment Freddy had lent them his Phaeton to come to the country, Jemima was determined that they should not turn to him for help again.

It had been difficult enough before, when she knew it was wrong to accept money they had no chance of repaying, but now when Freddy had said he loved her she thought it would be even more ignominious for them to take advantage of his generosity.

At the same time, because of what Freddy had said she felt a little warm glow in her heart that had not been there before.

She had been truthful when she had said she loved the Viscount, and it was something she had admitted to herself almost from the first moment she had married him.

She had only to see his handsome face and his slim, athletic body to feel her heart turn over in her breast.

But she told herself humbly that she was very, very lucky she could talk to him and look after him, and that should be enough.

Why should she ever hope that, loving anybody as beautiful as Niobe, he would ever notice her?

She was useful to him in seeing that he had three meals a day. And she had also provided him with the revenge he had longed to inflict on the woman who had cheated on him.

"Will that always be enough?" a voice asked Jemima as she told herself it would be greedy to ask for more.

She watched the Viscount and Freddy walking away after luncheon towards the stables to inspect the horses that were being broken in.

Then with a little sigh she started to clear the Dining-Room table.

"I'll do that for you, M'Lady," Hawkins said, coming in through the door which led into the Pantry.

"You must have your own luncheon first," Jemima replied. "There is a delicious ham which Mr. Hinlip brought, a pâté which I thought we could have again at dinner tonight, and an enormous sirloin of beef."

"I thought Mr. Hinlip wouldn't come empty-handed!"

"He has been very generous," Jemima said. "And what is more, he has sent his groom to the 'Green Man' so that we should not have to put him up."

"I'd heard that, M'Lady."

"We will get the room next to the Master's ready for him later," Jemima went on. "Old Mrs. Benson brushed it out yesterday, and if any of the old people are here this afternoon you could put them all in there to clean it up as best they can."

"I'll do that, M'Lady," Hawkins replied, "and Mrs. Groves is real handy at doing the washing up. Her legs are bad, so she prefers to do that rather than walk about the house."

"Then do let her do it," Jemima said, smiling.

She left Hawkins and thought she might join the men in the stables.

She had changed before luncheon into one of her London gowns and she looked down at it now a little doubtfully, wondering if she might damage it in any way and whether it would be better to change back into the dress she had been wearing when Freddy had first arrived.

Then she felt she could not bear him to see her looking so unfashionable, but in consequence it would be impossible for her to do any housework.

She tidied her hair in front of one of the mirrors, then set off towards the stables.

She thought, however, that it would be tactless to interrupt the friends too soon, so she did not go the quickest way out the front door and across what had once been a well-kept gravel sweep.

Instead she went through the West Wing of the house, a part of the Priory she had not yet had time to inspect.

It was of course very dusty, and she lifted her gown so that it would not touch the floor as she looked round her with interest, seeing in the rooms she passed pieces of furniture that might look better in those they were using.

Jemima had already made up her mind that the only sensible course would be to get the Drawing-Room and the Library looking as perfect as possible, and forget the rest of the house.

The Priory was so large that she had not had time since she arrived to see everything.

She had in fact had only a very quick look round and had begun to get two bedrooms and a Sitting-Room clean.

Now, she thought, in a week or so she would start changing things. Then if the Viscount really insisted on it, they would be able to receive their neighbours when they came to call on them.

She had walked quite a long way down the passage and realised she should be turning right to reach the stables.

She opened a door and found to her surprise that she was in a very strange-looking place and in it was a woman.

For a moment, because the woman had her back to the light, it was impossible to see her face. Then as Jemima moved forward the woman looked up, gave an exclamation, and curtseyed.

"I think you must be the new Viscountess Ockley," she said in a nervous but cultivated voice. "I do hope, My Lady, you will forgive me for being here without calling on you, but I did ask your manservant, and he said that His Lordship was not as yet receiving anyone."

The words seemed to fall over themselves in her anxiety to explain her presence, and Jemima smiled as she held out her hand.

"We have had rather a lot to do since we arrived," she said. "Will you tell me your name?"

"Of course, My Lady, I should have done so already! I am Mrs. Ludlow and my husband is the Vicar."

"I am delighted to meet you, Mrs. Ludlow."

The Vicar's wife was a middle-aged woman with a pleasant face and greying hair. She was dressed in a plain, old-fashioned gown and Jemima saw to her surprise that she had a large jug in her hand and on the floor there was another.

Mrs. Ludlow followed the glance of her eyes and said:

"I have come, My Lady, and perhaps it was wrong of me, without permission, to collect the

water. But I was sure His Lordship would not refuse it."

"Collect the water!" Jemima exclaimed in surprise.

"Yes, My Lady. There are those in the Parish
who feel they can't do without it, and when the
Vicar can spare me the pony and trap, I come and
fetch the water for them."

"What water, Mrs. Ludlow? I do not understand," Jemima said in a bewildered tone.

"It is there, My Lady," Mrs. Ludlow replied.

As she spoke she pointed, and Jemima saw now
why she had thought the room had looked so
strange.

In the centre of it was what appeared to be a
sunken hole surrounded by a stone circle almost
like a seat.

Although there was a raftered roof, the windows
had lost most of their glass, and that might have
been responsible for the moss and weeds which
were growing between the stones and in the hole.

Jemima stared down at it, trying to understand
what the Vicar's wife was talking about. Then she
saw a small trickle of water coming from between
the green weeds and accumulating in the centre.

There was a cup lying at the side and she realised that Mrs. Ludlow must collect the water once
there was enough of it in the centre and convey it
into the jugs she had brought with her.

"Why should you want this water?" she asked.
"Surely there must be water in the village?"

"Do you mean to say you haven't heard about
the water of Ockley Priory?" Mrs. Ludlow enquired. "Surely His Lordship . . ."

"His Lordship has never said anything to me about water," Jemima replied, "except that we have only just got the range in the kitchen to work."

"It is not that sort of water, My Lady. It is Holy Water—water in which the people in the village have such faith that they cannot live without it."

"Do tell me about it," Jemima begged.

"Well, it is a legend, of course," Mrs. Ludlow replied, "but the monks who built the Priory chose this particular site because their Abbott had a vision."

"What was it?"

"Our Lord appeared to him and told him he must heal the sick and the means of healing them would be given if he built the Priory on this spot."

"And he was referring to the water?"

"Yes, of course, My Lady, but I think it was forgotten about in the last century, or perhaps the Viscount Ockley at that time would not let the villagers use the spring."

Jemima smiled.

"But now they insist on helping themselves, or rather you take it to them."

"I think you will find that all your pensioners drink it as well," Mrs. Ludlow said. "In fact, everybody who lives in these parts talks about the water and the good it does them."

"What exactly does it do?" Jemima asked.

"First of all, they believe it keeps them young and active," Mrs. Ludlow replied, "and it certainly takes away the aches and pains in their legs. I can vouch for that myself. Last winter I was almost crippled with rheumatism, until the Vicar said to me:

" 'Why don't you drink the water, you silly woman? You fetch it for everybody else.' "

"What happened when you did?" Jemima asked.

"I have to admit I had never really believed in it myself," Mrs. Ludlow said in a low voice, as if she was frightened of being overheard. "Then within two weeks the pain in my legs grew less, and when I found it no longer difficult to climb the stairs, I realised I had been a 'doubting Thomas.' "

"So that is the story of the Holy Water," Jemima said with a smile.

She saw that there was now quite a pool of it in the centre of the hole.

"Does it ever run dry?" she asked.

"No, never, as far as I know," Mrs. Ludlow replied, "but it is very slow, and I think that is because the weeds are obstructing it. Perhaps it ought to be cleaned out."

"I must tell my husband about this," Jemima said. "But please take all you need, and perhaps I could talk to you about it another day."

"Yes, of course, My Lady. I should be very honoured," Mrs. Ludlow replied. "I hope His Lordship won't think it presumptuous of me to have collected the water without asking his permission."

"When I tell him that our neighbours need it, he will be delighted," Jemima answered.

She smiled at Mrs. Ludlow, then hurried out through the doorway, noticing as she did so that the door was off its hinges, and found herself not far from the stables but separated from them by a huge rhododendron hedge.

She found her way through it and discovered,

as she had expected, that the Viscount and Freddy
were not in the stables but looking at the horses
which had been let out by Hawkins into one of the
adjacent paddocks.

The grass was too long, the palings where they
had broken had been repaired in a very rough
fashion, but still the horses were enclosed and that
was what mattered.

"I call them Romulus and Remus," the Viscount was saying as Jemima joined them. "You will
remember they were wild children who were
adopted by a wolf, and I assure you, if I am to get
them into any sort of shape I shall have to be far
more fierce than any wolf!"

Jemima had hurried so quickly that she was almost breathless when she reached the Viscount's
side.

"Valient!" she said. "What do you think I have
just discovered?"

"If another ceiling has fallen, I do not wish to
hear about it!" he answered.

"No, it is nothing like that," Jemima said quickly.
"It is your well, the Holy Spring here in the Priory!"

The Viscount looked at her in surprise and she
knew for the moment that he did not know what she
was talking about. Then he exclaimed:

"Oh, I know what you are saying! There is a
spring at the end of the West Wing which is supposed to have magical powers. I remember my
grandfather telling me about it, but of course it is
a lot of moonshine!"

"That is not what the villagers think, and the

Vicar's wife told me it cured her rheumatism last year."

"Well, personally, I would rather drink the champagne Freddy has just brought us," the Viscount joked, "but everyone to his own taste!"

"It is not a joke!" Jemima said. "It is a discovery, and I think—in fact I am almost certain—that we have found what we have been looking for."

Because she spoke earnestly and seriously both men looked at her in surprise.

"What are you saying?" Freddy asked. "I have never heard of Valient having a Holy Spring, but I suppose one might expect something like that in a Priory."

"You are both being very unimaginative," Jemima said. "Listen—Mrs. Ludlow says that everybody in the village believes in it, and they make her come once or twice a week or whenever she can, to collect the water for them. The pensioners take it too, and when I think about it, I am surprised how well they look."

She saw that the Viscount was looking puzzled, as if he could not understand her enthusiasm, and she went on:

"You must be aware how popular Spas are? There are not only the famous hot-springs in Bath but the Beaulah Spa at Dulwich and the mineral-waters at Sadlers Wells.

She paused for breath before she went on:

"I remember years ago Papa and Mama going to Islington and telling me that when Lady Mary Wortley Montagu took a course of the waters, she found that while it was good for gout and arthritis, it made her very sleepy."

There was a moment's silence. Then the Viscount asked incredulously:

"Are you really suggesting we should open up a Spa here?"

"Why not?" Jemima replied. "If even only one person was cured, hundreds would want to come to drink the water, and they would be prepared to pay anything we asked, especially if it would not only relieve their pain but make them young again."

The Viscount stared at her in sheer astonishment, and Freddy exclaimed:

"My God—I believe Jemima has something! And the first persons who will be willing to drink it will be my mother, who has been suffering agonies for years with rheumatism, and my father, who grows more and more bad-tempered with his gout."

"Do you really think they would try it and tell us honestly what happens?" Jemima asked.

"Of course they would, if I asked them to do so. They have tried enough quack remedies one way and another, none of which has done them the slightest bit of good."

Jemima clasped her hands together.

"Supposing . . . just supposing what the Vicar's wife has told me is true—what do you think we could charge for the Ockley water?"

"As much as we can get!" the Viscount remarked.

Then he and Jemima smiled at each other, both

remembering that that was exactly what she had said to Mr. Roseburg.

"Come and look at it!" she said impetuously. "I think we shall have to clear the spring to make the water run faster, and tidy up the room . . . or perhaps it is a Chapel. But think how wonderful it would be if we could earn money and at the same time help people who are suffering."

"I think the whole idea is mad," the Viscount said, "but I am prepared to try anything."

Both men began to follow Jemima, who was walking away from them so quickly that they had to exert themselves to keep up with her.

"It will certainly be a new departure for you to be making money instead of spending it, Valient," Freddy teased.

"I shall expect you to help me," the Viscount answered. "I might even trust you to take the money at the door. I wonder if you ought to wear a uniform?"

Jemima had by now disappeared through the rhododendrons.

"I will tell you one thing," he added as he pushed his way through them, "unless I am convinced that this is a genuine way of making money, I am not going to waste a penny of mine or my valuable time on it."

"That is common sense," Freddy agreed. "At the same time, do not discourage Jemima. You must realise, Valient, that there is no other woman you have ever known, and I mean this, who would have done so much and so cleverly as she has done already, without complaint, and managing to enjoy every moment of it."

The way his friend spoke made the Viscount look at him in surprise. Then he said:

"Of course! You are right! I am very grateful to Jemima. She has worked like a Trojan this last week."

"Can you imagine Niobe in the same circumstances?" Freddy asked.

There was silence. Then as they neared the open door which led to the Holy Water, the Viscount said in a different voice:

"But of course Niobe would have no need to be subjected to the same circumstances as Jemima and I are in at the moment, would she?"

There was no reply that Freddy could make, but he wished that there was something he could say or do to make the Viscount aware that Jemima was undoubtedly a very exceptional, very unusual person.

Chapter Six

Jemima rushed along the passage and burst into the Sitting-Room, where the Viscount was standing at a table looking down at some piles of sovereigns.

"We have another twenty pounds!" she cried, waving a bag. "A whole coach-load of people arrived just as Freddy and I were closing up!"

The Viscount stared at her for a moment. Then he said:

"Do you know that means we have taken nearly ninety pounds today!"

He made a sound of triumph, then picked up Jemima under her arms as if she were a small child and swung her round and round, with her feet flying out as if she were a top.

"Ninety pounds!" he shouted. "Jemima, you are a clever, clever girl!"

He came to a standstill, still holding her off the floor, and kissed her on each cheek.

Then his lips touched hers.

It was only the kiss a man would give a child, but to Jemima it was as if a streak of lightning ran through her from her lips to her toes, and she felt a sudden, unexpressible rapture that was like nothing she had ever known before.

Then she was free and the Viscount took the bag of money from her hand to carry it to the table.

"Eighty-eight pounds five shillings!" he said in a wondering voice. "Is it possible?"

"You must . . . remember . . . this is the . . . first . . . day."

Jemima tried to speak in her ordinary voice, but it sounded strange even to herself and she knew it was because she was not only breathless from the way in which the Viscount had whirled her round, but also her body was still vibrating to the wonder of his lips.

"If they have come once they will come again," he said, "especially if it does as much good as Lady Hinlip says it does."

"Freddy's mother has been wonderful!" Jemima exclaimed. "We cannot be sufficiently grateful to her."

"I am indeed very grateful," the Viscount said positively, looking at the piles of money.

"Freddy says she has written dozens of letters to everybody in the County, and of course because the local newspapers reported what we were doing, that will bring in many more people."

"I still cannot believe it!" the Viscount said in a wondering tone.

Jemima felt that was not surprising.

All the time they had been repairing what she

now called the "Shrine" of the Holy Spring, she kept asking herself if it would really be as effective as she hoped and prayed.

They had all three together with Hawkins worked from early in the morning until late at night, and the Viscount had declared a dozen times that what he had endured in the Army was a rest-cure compared to being slave-driven by Jemima.

She first made them dig out all the weeds from the spring, which enabled the water to flow smoothly as it must have done when it was first built—and they discovered that when the sunken stone circle was full, the water seeped away naturally at the side so that it never overflowed.

Then they repaired the stones which surrounded the spring and cleaned them as best they could, and it was Jemima who found that one of the old pensioners was able to replace panes of glass in the windows.

After this she turned her attention to the walls.

They had been roughly plastered so that in many places the plaster was beginning to crumble and fall away, while it was also obviously very dirty.

"I think it would look much better," she said, "if we took the plaster off altogether and had just the bare walls. It would then look as it must have done when the monks first built it."

She pulled away a large piece of plaster as she spoke, then gave an exclamation.

"What is it?" Freddy enquired, looking up from what he was engaged in doing.

"Come here quickly!" Jemima cried. "I think I have found something!"

She had in fact found some very old murals which must have been painted centuries ago and which had doubtless been covered over by the Puritans.

It had taken them days of very hard work to remove the plaster without damaging the murals beneath it.

When they had done so, they found that they had three most delightful primitive drawings of saints surrounded by birds and small animals.

The colours had faded a little, and yet the soft muted shades seemed appropriate to the quiet atmosphere of the spring.

Where there were no more murals, the ancient stone of which the Priory itself had been built looked mellow and exactly right in what must originally have been a Chapel.

The Viscount found some carved wooden panels in the attics, which made a dado at the base of the murals, and they also searched until they discovered some oak chairs which seemed to fit in.

This had all taken time, but they had been tremendously encouraged in what they were doing when they received a report from Lady Hinlip on the effects of the spring-water which Freddy had taken to her.

She wrote to say that there was no doubt that her rheumatism had improved and she could move more easily. What was more, the inflammation in Lord Hinlip's foot, which had given him excrutiating pain, was definitely subsiding day by day.

"Now do you think the legend is a lot of moon-shine?" Jemima asked the Viscount.

"I take it all back," he replied, "and as you have made my back ache with all this hard work, I intend to drink the water myself, although I still prefer Freddy's champagne!"

"I have brought you two more cases, as it happens," Freddy said.

"You are too kind to us," Jemima told him.

Then as she saw the expression in his eyes, she knew why he had made no effort to go back to London and insisted on staying at the Priory, however uncomfortable it might be.

She was, however, very glad that he did so.

He kept the Viscount in a good temper and they all laughed a great deal despite the amount of work there was to be done.

As Jemima was determined that they would have their own Spa finished as soon as possible, there was very little time for the Viscount to train the horses or to ride Freddy's, which by now occupied several stalls in the dilapidated stables.

"The first thing we have to do when the shekels roll in," the Viscount said, "is to repair the roof."

"That is where you are wrong," Jemima said positively. "Before we spend any of the money on ourselves, we have to pay off our debts."

There was a rebellious expression on the Viscount's face, but before he could argue she said:

"It would be fair to go fifty-fifty at first because we have to live, but once that mill-stone round our necks is removed, there is so much that needs to be done, not only to the stables but also to the house."

The Viscount had made a hopeless gesture.

"Do you really think this mad idea is going to make us anything but a few sixpences?" he asked.

"I am prepared to bet that Jemima has found a gold-mine for you," Freddy replied loyally.

"I hope you are right," Jemima said, "but anyway it is worth a try."

Yet even the Viscount was impressed when they received the letter from Freddy's mother.

It was in fact Lady Hinlip who, because she had experience of so many Spas, told them what to charge and what they needed in the way of cans and flagons in which the water could be taken away.

They learnt that the Beaulah Spa at Dulwich, as did most other Spas, charged a subscription for a year of three guineas for a whole family, or one-and-a-half guineas per person.

It was also possible to buy the water at two shillings per gallon, or, for a souvenir, there were small flagons that could be purchased for a shilling.

Freddy offered to go to London to find out from the Spas where he could buy such things and when he came back, he had the further information that every Spa charged sixpence to drink the water.

Jemima did not forget Mrs Ludlow, who had said that the people in the village could not live without it, and the pensioners all thought it kept them young and active.

The first tickets they had printed were handed out free to everybody on the Viscount's Estate, and there was no doubt that because it was a novelty, a great number of people who had never before taken the water now came regularly to drink it.

There was not only the spring itself to be finished before it was opened to the public, but they also had to clear a driveway between the rhododendrons which had become very overgrown.

It was an exhausting job to put down barrow-loads of gravel outside the Spa to keep down the dust and, if it rained, the mud.

"Surely we could afford a labourer to do this?" the Viscount asked.

It was a very hot day and he and Freddy had wheeled barrowful after barrowful of gravel they had taken from a small pit which in the past had been used by the gardeners.

"How are·we to pay them?" Jemima asked pertinently.

Almost instinctively the Viscount had looked to where coming between the rhododendrons they could both see Freddy in his shirt-sleeves pushing an ancient wheel-barrow.

"No!" Jemima said firmly before he could speak. "You know as well as I do, Valient, how deeply in debt to him we are already."

"Freddy does not mind."

"That is not the point. This is your spring, your house, your Estate, and, if you like . . . your King-dom!"

There was a soft note in her voice as she said the last words and her eyes as she looked at her husband were very revealing.

The Viscount, however, was staring down at his blistered palms.

"All I can say," he said after a moment, "is that

if no-one drinks this damned water after all the trouble it has given me, I will throw you in the lake!"

"Unfortunately for you, I can swim!" Jemima retorted.

Because he sounded so irritable she walked away, praying frantically, as she had done every day, that the spring would be a success and she had not been foolish in suggesting they should open a Spa.

Now as she looked at the piles of money that the Viscount had been counting she knew it had exceeded her wildest expectations.

She was sensible enough to know that it was not only the spring that was a curiosity but so were both she and the Viscount to people who ordinarily would have ignored or laughed at Lady Hinlip's letter.

But they had driven up in their coaches and drunk from the small glasses that Jemima, wearing one of her prettiest gowns, had handed them with a smile.

The Viscount had greeted them in a very genial manner, looking extremely elegant in a spotless white cravat and his smartest champagne-coloured pantaloons.

It was only Hawkins and Jemima who realised that the unaccustomed manual work, having enlarged his muscles, had made his coat, always close-fitting, now too tight and if he exerted himself it might easily split at the seams.

Freddy was in the same position.

"My clothes are so constricting I can hardly

bear them," he said. "It must be all that delicious food you have cooked for us, Jemima!"

"You are responsible for a lot of it!" she replied with a smile.

"Only to save you from doing so much work," Freddy said. "I hate to see you working so hard."

He was always so considerate that she found herself wondering if the Viscount ever thought that she was doing an abnormal amount for a woman, especially one as small as herself.

There were breakfast, luncheon, tea, and dinner to be provided for men whose appetites seemed to increase every day!

Although Hawkins and the old women did their best in the house, it would not have been the same if Jemima had not arranged the flowers and, whenever she had a moment, mended the sheets and the pillow-cases.

Sometimes at night she would be so tired that she fell asleep as her head touched the pillow, and at others she was overtired and would lie awake wondering if the Viscount in the next room was still thinking of Niobe and yearning for her.

The one person Jemima was sure was never in his thoughts was herself.

He was pleasant to her, did what she asked, and appreciated the way she cooked, but she was quite certain that it had never for a moment struck him that she was his wife in the real sense of the word, nor that he might find her an attractive woman as Freddy did.

"I love . . . him! I love . . . him!" she whispered into her pillow.

Then when her heart ached and she thought

despairingly that she could never mean anything real or important to him, she chided herself for being ungrateful.

She could see him every day, hear him, and look after him, and although instinctively she wanted more, she was determined to be grateful for what she had already.

Sometimes she felt as if her mother were with her, guiding and helping her, and she was sure it had been her mother who had prompted her to enter the Chapel of the spring at exactly the right moment when Mrs. Ludlow was there.

Had she not been there, Jemima was sure she would have walked straight out through the open door and on to the stables without giving another glance at the sunken hole in the floor filled with weeds.

Looking at the money on the table now, she said:

"Somebody will have to go to London tomorrow to collect some more flagons and cans. We bought what seemed an enormous amount, but after the crowds today our store is very depleted."

"I noticed that everybody seemed to buy something," the Viscount remarked.

"I have thought of another idea," Jemima said.

"What now?"

"One of the ladies . . . I think it was the one you addressed as 'Betty,' asked if the lavender at the Priory was still as good as it used to be."

"That was Lady Cunningham," the Viscount explained. "I have known her ever since I was a child, and as she married a near neighbour they live about nine miles from here."

"What did she mean about the lavender?"

"It was always reputed to be exceptional because it smells stronger than the lavender other people have in their gardens."

"I have seen it!" Jemima exclaimed. "Although it is very overgrown with weeds, there is a great deal of it in what you told me was once the Herb-garden."

"We had better see whether the old men can do something about it," the Viscount suggested, "and now we will be able to pay them for any work they do."

"And if we get the old women like Mrs. Laing, who is skilful with her fingers, to make us lavender-bags," Jemima added, "we can put pot-pourri in others and sell them."

"Are you setting me up as a shop-keeper?" the Viscount asked.

"If you can sell water you can sell other things," Jemima answered. "You saw today how eager people were to have something to take away."

"I suppose you are right," he said somewhat reluctantly. "But I cannot remember when there was last an Ockley in trade."

"I expect if you go carefully through your family-tree you will find it difficult to come across an Ockley who was as poor as you are."

"That is true enough," he said soberly. Then with a quick change of tone: "Except for today, thanks to you, Jemima, I am feeling rich, and if Freddy does not appear soon with a bottle of champagne with which to celebrate, I shall open a case myself!"

"I would have been extremely obliged if you

had done so!" Freddy said from the doorway. "Although I now consider myself a master-carpenter, I have knocked my thumb on a nail getting the champagne open, and it is bleeding!"

"Then you must wash it," Jemima said quickly, "and I will bandage it for you."

"It is not as bad as that!" Freddy protested.

But already Jemima had hurried from the room to return with a small basin of cold water and a strip of linen.

She found that the Viscount and Freddy had already filled their glasses and as she came down the room towards them Freddy raised his.

"To a very astute little business-woman whom we love and admire!" he said.

The words were simple enough but the way he spoke them sounded, Jemima thought, somewhat indiscreet.

She glanced apprehensively at the Viscount, but she need not have worried, for he was pouring himself another glass of champagne and saying as he did so:

"I would never have believed, even if I were foxed, that a few cups of water would bring in so much money!"

"You were very sceptical when we started," Freddy said.

"You must admit it was a shot in the dark," the Viscount remarked, "and as I have just said to Jemima, I am the first Ockley who ever went into trade."

"I doubt if you will be the last," Freddy replied. "Times are changing. The days when every gentle-

man had a large fortune are, thanks to the war,
past."

"We have been lucky, very, very lucky," Jemima
said, "and, Freddy, if you are going to London
tomorrow, as you said you would, to fetch us some
more flagons, will you take part of this money to
Westons, the tailors, and say it is to be divided
amongst the other creditors?"

"You know I will do anything you want me to,"
Freddy said, "but I rather anticipate that as tomorrow is Sunday and we will have another huge in-
flux of visitors, I should be here to help you."

"Do you really think so?" Jemima asked. "I
thought Sunday, being a day of rest, people would
want to stay at home."

"I believe the Tivertons are coming over, for
one. They have a house-party, and my mother sent
me a message this afternoon which I have only just
had time to read, to say that if they could not get
here today they would come tomorrow."

"Then of course you must be here," Jemima said,
"and anyway, how idiotic of me! You can hardly
buy what we want in London on a Sunday!"

"Let us both go on Monday," the Viscount suggested.

Jemima gave Freddy a quick glance of alarm.

"That would be impossible!" he said quickly.

"Why?" the Viscount asked.

"You can hardly leave Jemima here alone."

The Viscount thought for a moment and Jemima
wondered if he was going to say that she could
look after herself. Then he said:

"No, I suppose you are right. You go, and if

you drop into the Club, tell them what we are doing. It will amuse them!"

"I could pin up a notice on the board saying you will welcome all those who are suffering from gout, and as there will doubtless be a large number you will give them a discount."

"You dare not do anything of the sort!" the Viscount cried. "And on thinking it over, it would perhaps be best not to mention it."

Freddy was about to make some reply when Hawkins came into the room carrying something in his hand.

"Is that the *Times,* Hawkins?" the Viscount asked.

"It came up from the village earlier this afternoon, M'Lord, but you was too busy for me to give it to you then."

"I have not seen a newspaper for days!" Freddy exclaimed. "I wondered when you were going to get round to ordering one!"

"I did that a week ago," the Viscount replied, "but things move slowly here and I can only hope that now we shall get a regular supply."

"I hope so too," Freddy answered. "We might be living on the moon for all we have heard of the outside world."

"If you ask me, it is rather a relief," the Viscount answered. "The newspapers are full of nothing but complaints about the Government, and reports of farming difficulties, to which I could add my own."

"I agree with you. There is nothing more depressing than the newspapers on everyday affairs,"

Freddy said. "The only time they cheer up is when there is a good war report."

"Thank goodness there is not one at the moment!" Jemima exclaimed.

She thought as she spoke how horrifying it would be if she now had to worry over the Viscound and Freddy fighting the French as they had done three years ago.

Whatever the difficulties they had to encounter, at least they were alive and safe.

Freddy filled up her glass of champagne, then his own.

He put down the bottle, then without saying anything raised his glass and drank to her a silent toast, his eyes very eloquent as he did so.

She turned her head aside quickly, feeling irritated that he must proclaim what he felt for her so obviously, and as she did so, the Viscount gave a sudden exclamation which seemed to echo round the room.

"My God!" he said. "What do you think has happened?"

"What is it?" Jemima asked.

"It is Porthcawl!" the Viscount answered, his eyes scanning the page as if he could hardly believe what he read.

"Porthcawl?" Freddy repeated. "What has he been up to?"

"He is dead!"

"Dead?"

"He had a heart-attack in the House of Lords. They carried him out of the Chamber, but he died before they could get him to his carriage and drive him home!"

"Good Heavens!" Freddy said. "But then he always looked a sickly sort of chap."

Jemima put down her glass and went from the room.

As she went slowly up the stairs she wondered what the Viscount was feeling.

Niobe had lost her first choice of a husband, and her second would have been available had he not been—married.

* * *

As Freddy had anticipated, the Spa the next day was besieged by visitors who obviously thought it was a new and interesting way of spending a Sunday afternoon.

Callers came from all over the County in their coaches, their Phaetons, their Chaises, and from the neighbouring villages farmers and their wives wearing their Sunday best drove over in their gigs and carts.

Most of them brought with them a very old mother or grandmother with fingers already gnarled with rheumatism and legs which found it hard to walk owing to arthritis.

Some of the elderly were so pathetic that as Jemima gave them the water to drink she prayed fervently that they would find it as effective as Lady Hinlip had done.

It was very reassuring to receive enthusiastic testimonials from the villagers who with their free cards had come to see the fun.

"Oi never left me bed, M'Lady, fer nigh on two year," one old woman told her, "but now, though 'tis a bit painful an' Oi gets twinges at toimes, Oi can make mesel' useful to me daughter an' even take a hand wi' th' washin'.''

"And you really think it is due to the water?"

"Oi'd swear it on th' Holy Bible, M'Lady! As Oi've said often enough, 'twas a gift from God Himself, an' who can say fairer than that?"

"Who indeed!" Jemima agreed.

There were of course a number of people who, having come a long distance to the Spa and having known the Viscount since he was a small boy, wanted to come into the house.

Jemima had begged him to say that they could not entertain visitors until they were more settled, but inevitably he was overruled and the neighbours were taken into the Drawing-Room.

Jemima felt uncomfortably that they were looking at the curtains that were faded, the carpets that were threadbare in places, and the cushions that wanted recovering.

But she thought the room looked beautiful! The furniture having been polished and the china dusted, it all seemed to fit in perfectly and be part of the mellow beauty of the Priory itself.

"I was a great friend of your husband's mother," one lady said to Jemima, "and I am so happy, my dear, that you and your husband have come to live at the Priory, and I hope we shall be friends too."

"That is kind of you, and I should like it very much," Jemima replied.

"You are just the sort of wife I hoped Valient would marry," the visitor went on. "I was always so afraid that he would become infatuated with one of those smart London girls who hate the country and who think of nothing but their looks and gowns."

She glanced round the Drawing-Room and said with a little smile:

"I can see that you have made things very homely, and that is what I think Valient needs now that the war is over. And no-one can say that the Priory is not big enough for a family of at least a dozen children."

Because the remark was unexpected, Jemima felt herself blushing, and the visitor gave a little laugh.

"I must not embarrass you, my dear. I shall tell Valient that I think he is a very lucky man, and as soon as your honeymoon is over you must both come and visit me."

Only when she had gone did Jemima find out that she had been talking to the Duchess of Newbury, one of the most influential personages in the whole County.

On Monday, when everything seemed a little flat, Freddy went off to London.

Although there was a trickle of visitors they arrived irregularly with gaps in between, so Jemima could not help wondering despairingly if the whole thing had been a "flash in the pan" and their new source of income had dried up already.

The same thing happened the next day, except that at about two o'clock in the afternoon two carriage-loads of people coming from some distance arrived.

Judging from the jovial mood they were in, they had obviously had something stronger than water to drink during their journey.

They all bought subscriptions for a year, although it seemed to Jemima unlikely that any of them would come again, and they purchased a dozen of the large jugs of the water and two dozen flagons before they left.

Because the Viscount had grown bored with hanging about waiting for customers, he had left Jemima alone.

There was no sign of him while she coped with the two carriage-loads. The men paid her extravagant compliments and would, she thought, had she given them the slightest encouragement, been flirtatious.

She was actually thankful that Hawkins was there, and because he took their glasses from them as soon as they had finished drinking, there was little excuse for them to hang about.

After a lot of banter they finally left, leaving the place strangely quiet after all the noise they had made.

"Why don't you have a bit of rest, 'M'Lady?" Hawkins suggested. "I'll be on duty, and if there's a big party I'll come and fetch you."

"I would feel as if I was deserting my post," Jemima replied, "but if you promise to fetch me . . ."

"I promise, M'Lady, and quite frankly, the beginning of the week is always slow and things pick up towards the end."

"How do you know that?"

"I've been talking to one of Mr. Hinlip's grooms, M'Lady, who's been to a lot of these Spas with His Lordship. He said they was all much of a muchness, and most of them were just

out to get all they could from those as patronised
them, while the water was no more miraculous
than if it had come out of a pump!"

"Oh, Hawkins, I am sure ours is not like that!"

"Of course not, M'Lady. You heard what Lady
Hinlip said about it? That's the sort of testimonial
we wants."

"That is what I thought," Jemima agreed.

"In fact, I were thinking, M'Lady," Hawkins
went on, "it'd be a good idea if you wrote down
what these people say, an' of course Mr. Hinlip's
mother and father. You could get it printed and
either give it away, or, if Your Ladyship wrote it
in with a history of the Priory, I dare say a lot of
people would buy it."

Jemima stared at him for a moment, then clapped
her hands.

"Hawkins, you are a genius! Of course that is
what we could do! Why did I not think of it myself?"

"The idea comes to me, M'Lady, when I were
talking to old Mrs. Burns. The claims she makes
about the water you'd find it hard to believe, but
she believes them!"

"She will be working in the house tomorrow
morning, and I will get her to tell me exactly what
she told you," Jemima said. "Then there are all
the other old people, of course, and Mrs. Ludlow,
who could tell me who to talk to in the village."

She gave a little cry of delight, and her eyes
were shining as she said:

"This is a new idea and I must tell His Lordship
about it."

As if she could not stop to walk in a dignified

manner, she picked up the front of her gown and entered the house the way she had come the first time.

She ran along the passage, which, now that it was in regular use, had been cleaned and dusted, as had the furniture and paintings on either side of it.

Jemima was in a hurry and she ran until she reached the Hall. Then she released her gown as she walked towards the Drawing-Room.

Only as she got to the door and before she opened it did she put up her hands to smooth her hair into place, when she heard voices.

She wondered who could be talking to the Viscount and looked back at the front door, which was open.

It was then that she saw there was a closed carriage outside and felt that it must be yet another neighbour who was calling on them! She was just about to walk into the Drawing-Room when something about the carriage seemed familiar.

A second later she recognised the colour in which it was painted and the elaborate crest on the door.

She felt as if a cold hand clutched at her heart. Then, drawing in her breath as if to give herself courage, she turned the handle of the Drawing-Room door.

She opened it slowly because she was apprehensive and a little afraid. Then as she heard her own name mentioned she was suddenly still.

"You only married Jemima to spite me," Niobe was saying, "and, Valient, I am deeply ashamed of the way I treated you."

"It is rather late for that," the Viscount answered.

"I was sorry as soon as you had gone."

There was a beguiling note in her soft voice which Jemima knew she could assume so cleverly when it suited her.

"Papa forced me to say I would marry the Marquis," Niobe went on. "I pleaded with him, I begged him, saying that I loved you, but he would not listen."

She made a sound that was curiously like a sob.

"You know how overbearing and dictatorial Papa is, and I was too frightened to disobey him."

There was no reply from the Viscount and Niobe went on:

"But please believe me, Valient, you must believe that I have loved you for along time, and you cannot imagine I ever wanted to marry the Marquis when he was so old and ill? I wanted you— you! As I want you now!"

Jemima drew the door quietly to, knowing she could not bear to listen to any more.

She turned to walk very slowly across the Hall to the stairs, and she went up them as if she had suddenly grown as old and decrepit as some of the women who had come to the Spa.

When she reached her bedroom she went to the window to sit down in the window-seat and stare with unseeing eyes out over the Park.

She knew from what she had overheard that her whole world, that small, very precious world she had built in the last few weeks, had fallen in ruins round her.

Now she was of no further use to the Viscount but only an encumbrance, and everything he wanted, everything he desired, was within reach, except that she stood in the way.

"What shall I do?" she asked herself.

Then because she loved him the question changed.

"How can I help him? How can I make him happy?"

She knew as she spoke that there was only one way, and it was very obvious.

She must go out of his life in the same unexpected and unpredictable manner in which she had entered it.

The question was—how?

For one moment Jemima thought that she might run away with Freddy as he had asked her to do. But she knew that that would only discredit the Viscount in the eyes of his friends and neighbours who had accepted her so graciously when they had come to the Priory on Saturday and Sunday.

She could be divorced, but she had the feeling that Niobe would not wait for the Viscount to be free if someone more important than he were to come along in the meantime.

What was more, a divorce took a long time going through Parliament, and that meant that Valient would have nothing to live on while he was waiting to marry his rich bride.

'I have to die!' Jemima thought.

She remembered how on the day they had come to the Priory they had said that if things went wrong, they could always drown themselves in the lake.

'Unfortunately, I can swim!'

She remembered that she had said this to the Viscount and she also knew that if she was to die, it must not be on his doorstep so that he might be held responsible.

She put her hand up to her forehead.

"I have to ... think! I have to ... think!" she told herself under her breath.

Her head felt like cotton-wool and it was impossible for her to sort things out. She could only remember the soft, seductive tone in Niobe's voice as she told the Viscount that she loved him.

Jemima knew only too well what her cousin was looking like as she spoke—the clarity of her pink-and-white skin, the perfection of her features!

And the loveliness of her blue eyes that could look, when she wanted them to, so alluring, so sincere, and so truthful, even when she was lying.

"Valient loves her! He loves her!"

Her heart seemed to be beating out the words against her breast.

Of course he loved her. She was the most beautiful girl he had ever seen, and she was also rich.

The Priory could be restored to its former glory and there would be no need to take money for the Holy Spring. It could be free for everybody who believed it would help them.

Valient's debts could be paid off and he and Niobe could live in Berkeley Square when they were in London and give Receptions, Balls, and dinner-parties where the food would be superlative and the waiting would be done by experienced servants because they could afford to pay the highest wages.

"He could have it all tomorrow ... at once ... the next day ... if I was ... not here."

Jemima whispered the words. Then she knew that every nerve in her body was crying out against leaving the man she loved.

She would have nothing without him and she knew that she would rather be dead than face a future alone.

"I will die ... I will ... die somehow," Jemima told herself.

What was the point of love, she argued, if one was not prepared to make the greatest sacrifice of all for the person one loved?

She knew that the way she loved Valient was with her whole heart and soul, and to sacrifice her body for him was really of little importance.

"I will die!" she said again.

Then she could feel her mother beside her and the feeling was so vivid, so real, that she felt she only had to turn to see her there.

There was no need to ask what her mother was saying.

Jemima knew the answer.

It was that it was wicked to take a life that had been given by God, however hard it might be to go on living.

Jemima shut her eyes and when she tried to pray her mother was still there, speaking to her, comforting her, and guiding her.

It was then, almost as if she could hear her speaking that she knew what she must do.

Chapter Seven

"What did Niobe say then?" Freddy insisted for the hundredth time.

"She told me that her father had forced her to marry the Marquis," the Viscount replied. "She had pleaded with him, begged him, saying that she loved me, but he would not listen."

Freddy made a derisive sound but did not speak, and the Viscount went on:

"She then said she was frightened to disobey Sir Aylmer, but she had loved me for a long time and how could I imagine she wanted to marry the Marquis when he was so old and often ill."

There was silence. Then Freddy, although he had heard it all before, asked:

"What did you answer?"

"I did not answer for a long time," the Viscount replied, "because I was thinking, strange though it seemed, that Niobe no longer attracted me."

He got up from the chair as he was speaking and

walked about the room in a restless fashion, as if it echoed his thoughts.

"It is difficult to put into words what I did feel," he went on after a moment. "I was so sure that I loved Niobe as I had never before loved any woman in my life, because she was so beautiful. But suddenly, in a way I cannot understand, her beauty had less effect on me than if she had been a stone statue."

"I always felt like that about Niobe," Freddy said, "but what I think is immaterial. Go on with what happened."

"I suppose I must have been staring at her in a strange fashion," the Viscount said, "finding it almost inconceivable that when I had thought I loved her so desperately and it was something which would last for eternity, she suddenly meant nothing more to me than one of those old women who come to drink the water."

He walked across the room and back again before he continued:

"Niobe must have realised something was wrong, because she said:

" 'I love you, Valient, and I know you love me. We must do something about it.'

"She would have put her arms round my neck, but I turned away from her and said:

" 'It is far too late, Niobe. I am a married man, and we actually have nothing to say to each other.' "

"That must have surprised her!" Freddy said beneath his breath.

"I think she gave a little scream," Valient said.

"Then she was close against me, her face turned up to mine, as she said:

" 'Divorce Jemima. Have the marriage annulled. Papa will be able to arrange that, and we can be together as we were meant to be.' "

The Viscount paused.

"It was when she mentioned her father that I realised what the two of them were up to, and I told Niobe what I thought of her and her father! I can assure you, after what I said they will neither of them speak to me again!"

"Thank God for that!" Freddy said. "What we have to determine now is what Jemima was doing."

"Hawkins says that she left the spring to tell me some new idea he had suggested to her."

"Yes, I know," Freddy remarked, "and that means she must have come to the Drawing-Room when Niobe was with you."

"And you think," the Viscount said slowly, "that she overheard Niobe saying she loved me, and did not wait to hear my reply?"

"That is the only possible explanation for the way she disappeared," Freddy said.

They had been going over the same ground for over a week.

At first Valient had thought that after Niobe had called at the house, he had managed to send her away without anyone else being aware that she had been there.

Then when Hawkins brought him the money after he had closed the spring, he had asked:

"Do you know where Her Ladyship is, M'Lord? It's getting late and she hasn't started to prepare the dinner yet."

"I thought she was with you," the Viscount answered.

"No, M'Lord, she left me early in the afternoon, at about three o'clock, I think it was."

"I expect she has gone to lie down and has no idea of the time," the Viscount said lightly. "Go and knock on her door, Hawkins, and wake her."

"I'll do that, M'Lord," Hawkins answered.

He had returned a few minutes later to say that Jemima was not in her room nor could she be found anywhere else in the house.

The Viscount had not been worried. The newspaper had come and he settled down to read what was happening in London, thinking as he did so that while he had no intention of telling Jemima that her cousin had called, he would certainly relate to Freddy everything that had occurred.

However, he found himself not reading the newspaper but instead thinking how strange it was that quite suddenly, for no reason he could possibly ascertain, Niobe had lost all her attraction for him.

When he had thought of her, which at first was continually, then not as frequently when he had been so busy, she had always seemed to be surrounded by a cloud of glamour which was irresistible.

Today she had appeared ordinary, almost common-place, and although he was still perfectly prepared to admit that she was exceedingly beautiful, it was a beauty which no longer attracted him as a man.

"How can this have happened so suddenly?" he asked himself, and wondered if Freddy would have an explanation.

When Freddy arrived the following day it was to find the Viscount annoyed, irritated, and at the same time anxious about Jemima.

"She has just disappeared, Freddy," he said. "She never came back to cook dinner, she did not sleep here last night, and nobody has any idea what can have happened to her."

It was Freddy who had discovered, from what Hawkins had said about her leaving him to find the Viscount, that when she reached the Drawing-Room Niobe must have been inside.

When he heard the Viscount's account of what had occurred, he knew that that was why Jemima had left and he thought it seemed unlike her not to be brave enough to stay and face the music.

It was then that the two men found they had not the slightest idea where Jemima, having left the Priory, would be likely to go.

"What money would she have with her?" Freddy asked.

"I have no idea," the Viscount replied. "I presume she had the two guineas that she brought with her when she left her uncle's house, and she had taken some of the money we made from the spring on the first day to pay the bill we owed in the village-shop."

"What happened to the rest?" Freddy enquired.

"I paid Hawkins's wages and the accounts for the cans and flagons and for the materials we needed for repairs. The rest is in my desk."

"That means Jemima will not have been able to go very far. Has she any relatives apart from Sir Aylmer?"

"She certainly would not go to her uncle," the

Viscount said positively, "and she told me the first day we met that if she went to any of her other relations they would be so frightened of him that they would refuse to keep her."

"Then where the devil could she be hiding?" Freddy asked.

"I have gone over in my mind almost everything she ever said to me," the Viscount said. "She never mentioned any friends or an old Nurse or Governess for whom she had any affection."

"We can hardly go to London and walk about the streets looking for her," Freddy said helplessly.

"That is what I was thinking last night, when I could not sleep," the Viscount admitted. "Do you think I ought to ask Sir Aylmer if he has heard anything from her?"

"I am absolutely positive he is the last man on earth she would turn to for protection," Freddy replied. "You know how he treated her, and anyway, seeing the way she heard Niobe talking to you, it is not likely that she would throw herself on the mercy of her cousin."

"No, of course not," the Viscount agreed. "But what can we do? Where can we look?"

It was a cry he repeated day after day as he and Freddy waited, hoping against hope that Jemima would come back.

They agreed that it would be a tremendous mistake for anyone except themselves to know that she had vanished.

When the neighbours came to drink the water of the spring and made excuses to come into the house, the Viscount merely said that his wife was lying down, or that she had gone out for the afternoon, and promised that next time they called she would be delighted to meet them.

"We cannot go on like this," Freddy said savagely.

The days seemed to crawl by and nothing seemed the same without Jemima there.

The attendance at the Spa seemed to be increasing rather than diminishing, but the Viscount ceased to be excited about the money they were making and on several evenings he did not even bother to tot it up.

The difference in the food was very apparent, despite the hams and pâtés that Freddy had sent from his own home, and even the champagne they drank while they were talking about Jemima seemed less palatable than it had in the past.

"We have to do something," Valient said suddenly. "I am going to call in the Bow Street Runners."

As Freddy opened his lips to expostulate, the door opened and Hawkins came into the room.

"I'm sorry not to have brought you this earlier, M'Lord," he said, "but I've been so busy at the spring I couldn't get away."

"What is it, Hawkins?"

"A letter, M'Lord."

"I suppose it is another invitation," the Viscount said as he took it from his valet. "God knows what excuse I can make this time as to why Jemima and I cannot attend the dinners given by our over-hospitable neighbours."

"They want to meet her," Freddy said, "and so do we."

"Excuse me, M'Lord," Hawkins interrupted, "but

Emily's here, and I thought Your Lordship might like to have a word with her."

"Emily?" the Viscount queried.

"You remember her, M'Lord. The house-maid as worked for us in Berkeley Square. Mr. Roseburg took her on when he moved in."

"Oh yes—Emily!" the Viscount exclaimed. "Of course I would like to see her and hear what is happening in London."

"What is she doing here if she works for Ròseburg?" Freddy asked.

"Her father and mother live in the village, Sir," Hawkins explained, "and Emily came up here almost as soon as she arrived, hoping to see Her Ladyship. Very fond of her, she was."

The Viscount looked at Freddy meaningfully before he said:

"I will see her in a few minutes, Hawkins. I expect you have given her a cup of tea?"

"She's been helping me at the spring, M'Lord, but now that it's shut, we'd both appreciate something to eat."

"When you have had it, bring Emily along to me," the Viscount ordered.

"Very good, M'Lord."

"I was just wondering," the Viscount said as the door shut behind his valet, "whether Emily might have an idea of where Jemima would go."

"The same thought crossed my mind," Freddy admitted.

"I remember Jemima liked Emily," the Viscount went on, "while she had no use for the Kingstons, and with reason."

As he was talking, he casually opened the letter

he held in his hand. Then as he read it, he exclaimed:

"Oh, my God! It cannot be true!"

"What is it?" Freddy asked.

The Viscount did not reply but merely handed the letter to his friend, then walked across the room to stand staring out the window with unseeing eyes.

There was something in the way the Viscount had spoken which made Freddy anticipate what he would read.

He stared down at the letter:

My Lord:

It is with deep regret that I write to inform Your Lordship that I was called several days ago to minister to a young woman who was dying of smallpox. Nothing could be done to to save her life, but before she died she told me that her real name was the Viscountess Ockley, and she asked me to inform Your Lordship of her demise.

She died soon after I had spoken with her, and the body, as is usual to avoid infecting others, was buried as quickly as possible.

I can only express to Your Lordship my sympathy and commiseration in what must be a sad loss.

I remain, Your Lordship, your most obedient and respectful servant,

John Brown. Curate.

Freddy read the letter through, then read it again.

Then as he stared at the paper he held in his hand, the Viscount said:

"So—she is dead!"

There was silence for a moment. Then Freddy ejaculated:

"I do not believe it!"

"What do you mean—you do not believe it?"

"It is too pat, too obvious a solution to your problem."

"What problem?" the Viscount enquired.

Freddy had risen and was standing with his back to the fireplace as he went on:

"Jemima overhears Niobe saying that she loves you and she believes that you love her. She disappears and she knows the only way you can be free of her is by her death. So she dies—or at least she is determined that we shall think she has!"

"Are you telling me this is a lie?" the Viscount enquired.

Freddy held out the letter to him.

"Look at it. What do you think is strange about it?"

The Viscount took the letter from him and read it again.

Then he exclaimed:

"There is no address, for one thing!"

"That is what I noticed," Freddy said, "and the person who wrote it, apart from having the most ordinary name—there may be dozens of 'John Browns' in Holy Orders—is also merely a Curate."

"What does that signify?" the Viscount enquired.

"Only that he would be far more difficult to trace than if he were a Vicar or a Rector. I imagine it would be easy to trace a Vicar at a Church within a radius of thirty to fifty miles from here, but a Curate, especially one called John Brown, is almost untraceable."

"I see what you mean."

"And smallpox is a very convenient disease," Freddy went on. As the writer of this letter says, they bury the body quickly so that it cannot infect other people."

"But why—why would Jemima do this?" the Viscount enquired.

"Because she loves you!" Freddy replied savagely.

"She loves me?" the Viscount repeated. "How do you know?"

"Because she told me so."

"Why should she have done that?"

"If you want the truth," Freddy answered, "it was because I asked her to come away with me!"

The Viscount looked stupefied from sheer astonishment. Then he said slowly, emphasising every word:

"*You* asked Jemima—my wife—to come away with you? I thought you were my friend!"

"I was not trying to take from you anything you wanted yourself," Freddy replied. "I love Jemima, I have loved her from the first moment I saw her, and if you want the truth, Valient, I find it agonising to watch her slaving after you, obeying your every wish, trying to make you happy, when you were hardly aware that she even existed."

"If any other man had said to me what you have just said," Valient said, "I would knock him down!"

"Oh, for God's sake, Valient," Freddy ejaculated, "do not play the Cheltenham dramatics with me!

You know as well as I do that you did not care a tinker's curse for Jemima before she disappeared."

"I suppose that is true," the Viscount said reluctantly. "It was only when she was gone and I was aware what a difference she had made to this place and that I missed her laughter, that now I keep thinking how damned quiet it is."

He suddenly gave a cry that seemed to echo round the room.

"I will tell you one thing, Freddy. If she is alive, as you say she is, I am going to find her! She has to come back—she has to! I might have known that double-faced Niobe would mess up my life in one way or another."

"That is true enough, but whatever Niobe has done or not done, you still have to find Jemima."

"I will find her!" the Viscount said definitely. "I feel it in my bones, as my Nanny used to say, and when I find her I will thank you to remember, Freddy, that she is *my* wife!"

"I am prepared to do that," Freddy answered, "as long as it is something you remember yourself."

"Any more of your damned impertinence..." the Viscount began, but before he could say any more, the door opened.

"Here's Emily, M'Lord," Hawkins announced.

* * *

Jemima finished the prayer which the children had repeated after her line by line. Then she went to sit at the ancient harmonium which stood against the wall.

"Who is going to choose the hymn this morning?" she asked.

The children, whose ages ranged from three to nine, crowded round her.

"What about *All Things Bright and Beautiful?*" one of the older girls suggested.

"That is a good idea!" Jemima said. "And you all know that one."

She struck the first chord on the wheezy harmonium and the children drew in their breaths so as to be able to make as much noise as possible.

It was the Vicar who had suggested, when Jemima went back to the village where she had lived with her father and mother, that she should occupy herself in teaching in the "Penny a Week" School that had just been started in the village.

The old teacher, who was a retired Governess, had died. The children were rapidly forgetting everything she had taught them, and there was no chance of their attending any sort of School within a radius of many miles.

Jemima had been certain as she journeyed to Lower Maidwell that it was the only place where she would find someone to help her.

It was a journey which, although not very long across country, necessitated her changing coaches three times.

Finally after a very uncomfortable night in a cheap Coaching-Inn she had arrived at the village on the following morning and had gone at once to the Vicarage.

There she found the old Vicar, who had been

fond of both her father and her mother. When Jemima told him how unhappy she had been with her uncle and how harshly he had treated her, he agreed that she had been wise to leave.

"But I have to find somewhere to live," Jemima said, "and I must try to earn a little money."

The Vicar suggested that the old woman who had cleaned for her father and mother might have a room in her cottage. Then he suddenly exclaimed that he was sure everyone would be delighted if she would take on the teaching of the children.

"You will not get rich, Jemima, from the pennies your pupils pay you," he said, "but there is a little money in the Poor Fund that I can allocate to you, and perhaps later something else might turn up that you could do in the afternoons."

"I am very grateful for your kindness, Vicar," Jemima said, "and I would love to teach the children."

"Do not say that until you have seen them!" the Vicar begged. "They behave, I am told, extremely badly in Sunday-School, and I find myself shouting in Church above the noise they make during my Sermon!"

Jemima knew this was because once he got into the pulpit the Vicar was very long-winded, and while the older members of his congregation simply went to sleep, the younger ones would play games at the bottom of the pews.

But she was so glad to find that there was somewhere she could stay and something she could do that for a moment her misery and unhappiness at leaving the Viscount lightened a little.

Because she missed him unbearably it was impossible for her thoughts not to keep returning to him and to the Priory and she wondered almost every minute of the day what was happening now that she had left.

The idea of making the Viscount believe she had died was, she believed, the only possible way in which he could be set free, short of actually killing herself.

That would not only be a difficult thing to carry out, but every instinct in her body shrank, even though she was so desperately unhappy, from taking her own life.

"I love him," she told herself, "and although ... everything is ... dark and empty ... without him, I at least have my ... memories."

There were memories of what he had said, how he had looked, and that one magical moment when after he had swung her round like a child he had kissed her first on both cheeks, then on her lips.

She was fully aware that it had meant nothing to him, but she knew it was something which she would never forget and which was engraved on her heart so that whatever happened in the future, that was hers forever.

The days were not so difficult to endure because she was kept busy, and it was almost like being back at the Priory to have to clean out the School which was at the back of the Vicarage and which since the last teacher's death had been used as a store-room.

It was dusty, full of cobwebs, and there was a whole variety of broken china, garden implements, cans, and bits of sacking that had to be carried away before the floor could be scrubbed.

There was no-one to help Jemima because the Vicar, being a widower, only employed one old woman as his Housekeeper who was past doing anything except her duties in the house.

Jemima could in fact have asked for help from one of the fathers of her future pupils, but because she did not wish to have time to think, she found that working helped her for a few minutes at any rate to forget the Viscount.

It also made her so tired that she could sleep when she got to bed.

But once her manual work was over, the nights were sheer misery when her love became a physical and mental agony that felt at times as if she had a thousand daggers embedded in her heart and the pain of them was unbearable.

She had always imagined that love was something beautiful which gave one a sense of security and protection.

But a love that was lost was very different. It was just a continuing torture which seemed to intensify day after day, night after night.

Sometimes Jemima would think that she had been crazy not to have run away with Freddy when he had asked her to do so.

They could have gone abroad and the Viscount would have divorced her. Perhaps eventually, when he married Niobe, Freddy and she would have been married.

But Jemima knew if she had done that she would have destroyed her own ideals, and it would have hurt not only Freddy but also the Viscount.

How could she create a scandal for either of them?

What was more, she knew that although she was very fond of Freddy and he would always have a small place in her heart, she could never make him the wife he deserved, when she loved the Viscount with every breath she drew.

When she had written her letter saying she had died of smallpox, she had thought that it was an entirely reasonable explanation of what might have happened.

Having written it, she had waited until there was a Carrier going from Lower Maidwell to London and had asked him to post it from there.

She had paid him for doing so, and as she looked at the small amount of money she had, she had the thought that she must be very economical.

Old Mrs. Barnes, in whose cottage she was staying, fortunately charged her only two shillings sixpence a week for her lodging and the same amount for her food.

It was plain fare, but while it was very different from the dishes Jemima could cook herself, she asked for nothing more.

She was never hungry and, as Mrs. Barnes said over and over again, did not eat enough food to keep a mouse alive.

"Perhaps I will waste away like the heroine of some novelette," Jemima told herself.

She realised that she had grown very thin and the two gowns she had brought with her in the small valise which was all she could carry were already far too large round the waist.

She had left behind all her elegant gowns that had been bought in London and it never struck her that because they were still hanging in the wardrobe of her bedroom, the Viscount was convinced she would return.

"What woman ever goes anywhere without her clothes?" he asked Freddy. "Do you remember that creature who attached herself to us in France and who by the end of the campaign had a dozen pieces of baggage travelling with the Quartermaster's stores?"

"You can hardly compare her with Jemima!" Freddy growled.

"No, of course not, but she was a woman! And Jemima was so pleased with her clothes when we bought them for her."

"She looked lovely in them!" Freddy muttered, but beneath his breath so that the Viscount did not hear.

Jemima from one point of view did not miss her clothes.

She had worn them because she wanted to look attractive in the Viscount's eyes, but she always had the uncomfortable feeling that he would not have noticed if she had on sackcloth and ashes!

What did worry her, when she thought about it, was how she would ever be able to replace the clothes she did have when they were worn out.

Even if she made her gowns herself, as she had done before, they would still cost money.

She remembered that the Vicar had said he would try to find her something else to do besides teaching in the School, and she thought that after a month she would not seem impatient if she reminded him of his promise.

In the meantime the children occupied her mornings and she enjoyed teaching them, finding after a few tussles at the beginning that they responded to what she asked of them and were on the whole extremely well behaved.

She wished she did not have to take the pennies the parents paid for their children to be educated, but she knew they would think it strange if she refused to do so.

Besides, there was no use pretending she did not need the money herself.

In some Counties the Squire and the Parishioners would pay for a School-teacher so that the children's education was free, but Lower Maidwell was a poor village and there were no wealthy landlords in the vicinity.

The hymn came to an end and the "Amen" roared out with all the strength that fifteen pairs of lungs could muster.

Jemima rose and shut the lid of the harmonium.

"That is all for today, children. Be here punctually at ten o'clock tomorrow morning and try to remember what you have learnt so far."

"We will, Miss! Good-day, Miss!"

Because Jemima had taught them to do so, the boys bowed and the girls curtseyed.

Then they clattered out through the door and she could hear them shouting and laughing as they ran down the path which led to the village street.

Jemima went to the rickety table which served

as a desk and stacked together the books that were lying on it.

She was thankful to find that the teacher before her had left the easy primers which she had used to teach her pupils through the long years she had taught in private service.

The books were old and some of them were obviously out-of-date, but, with no money to buy any more, Jemima was thankful to have them.

She picked them up in her arms and carried them to where behind her was a cupboard. The doors were open and she put the books inside on a shelf.

As she did so, she heard footsteps approaching the door which was open and which led to the garden.

She thought it was the old man who grew vegetables for the Vicar and sometimes left his tools in the School-Room so that they could be locked up until he came the next day.

"I am just going, Mr. Jarvis," Jemima said, without turning round.

She shut the cupboard door as she spoke, and, thinking it strange that Mr. Jarvis, who was usually very garrulous, did not reply, she looked over her shoulder.

Then she gave a little exclamation.

Standing in the School-Room, looking somehow overpoweringly large and at the same time very elegant, was the Viscount.

For a moment Jemima could not move and her voice seemed to have died away in her throat. It was almost as if the same thing had happened to the Viscount, for he just stood looking at her.

Then at last, in a whisper he could barely hear, Jemima asked:

"H-how ... how did you ... f-find ... me?"

As if she broke the spell, the Viscount walked towards her, saying as he did so:

"How could you run away in that damnable fashion? How could you send me that outrageous letter saying you were dead?"

He sounded so angry that Jemima trembled, and yet at the same time her heart was singing irrepressibly because he was there.

She was looking at him, seeing him! And while she had thought that never again would she hear his voice, he was speaking to her.

He stood in front of her and she knew he was waiting for an answer.

"I ... I thought ... it was ... b-best," she faltered.

"For me?"

"I knew ... you would ... want to be ... free."

"You might at least have asked me what I wanted."

"I ... I did not ... have to ask ... I heard what N-Niobe said to you."

"While you were so busy eavesdropping," the Viscount retorted, "you might have waited to hear my answer to her ridiculous assertions!"

He saw Jemima's eyes widen. Then he asked:

"What have you been doing to yourself? You are much thinner!"

"I ... I am ... all right."

"That is more than I am," the Viscount replied. "Have you any idea of the havoc you have caused by going off in that mad fashion? Freddy and I have not had a decent thing to eat since you left, and we have talked about you until, if your ears were not burning, they blasted well should have been!"

Jemima clasped her hands together. Then she said in a very small voice:

"Do you . . . mean . . . you minded my . . . leaving?"

"Minded?" the Viscount's voice rose. "Of course I minded! If I were an uncivilised man like your uncle I would give you a good beating for running away without telling me where you were going and for sending me an untruthful letter saying you were dead and nearly causing me to call in the Bow Street Runners at enormous expense."

Jemima gave a cry of horror.

"Oh, Valient, you did not do that? I know they are very expensive."

"The money did not matter as long as I could find you."

His eyes met Jemima's and now it seemed as if he was no longer angry but looking at her in a way which made her heart begin to beat very quickly.

Because she dared not trust the strange feeling that was sweeping over her, she said:

"I am . . . sorry. Very . . . very . . . sorry if I have been a . . . nuisance. I was only . . . trying to make you . . . happy."

"Well, you only succeeded in making me feel anxious, frustrated, and cursed miserable."

"I did not . . . mean to do . . . that. I thought you would . . . want to marry Niobe . . . and that was the only way you could . . . do so."

"As I have already said," the Viscount answered, "if you had listened a little longer at the key-hole you would have heard me tell Niobe what I thought of her and add that I had no wish ever to see her again."

Jemima drew in her breath.

"You . . . really said that to . . . Niobe?"

"That, and a great deal more," the Viscount replied with a note of relish in his voice. "I can promise you one thing—we will neither of us be troubled by your cousin or your uncle in the future."

"B-but I was . . . sure you . . . loved her."

"I thought I did," the Viscount admitted frankly, "but I was wrong—very, very wrong."

He saw the light that came into Jemima's eyes before he said:

"Before I say any more, I want you to tell me why you were so concerned for my happiness. I may not have been a very good husband, Jemima, but I did give you a home which you told me you appreciated, and I cannot believe you prefer being here to living at the Priory."

"No . . . of course not! You know that I . . . love the Priory . . . and I . . . loved being . . . there."

There was silence. Then the Viscount asked:

"And is there nothing else you love besides the house?"

Jemima drew in her breath. Then her eyes fell before his and he saw the colour rise in her pale cheeks.

"I want you to answer that question, Jemima, and it is very important that you should be truthful."

He saw a little quiver run through her. Then as if she was frightened by what he was asking her, she trembled as she turned away from him.

He reached out his arms and held on to her.

"Answer me! Answer me, Jemima! Tell me what else you love besides my house!"

There was a note in his voice which seemed to vibrate through her, and now slowly she raised her eyes to his and saw the expression in his grey ones, which made her feel as if her heart turned a somersault and went on turning.

He drew her a little closer.

"Tell me—please tell me, Jemima," he pleaded. "I want to hear you say it."

"I . . . I . . . love . . . you!"

The words were so faint that he could barely hear them.

"That is what I wanted you to say," the Viscount exclaimed, "because, my darling, although it is rather late in the day, I love you!"

As he spoke, he pulled her against him and his lips came down on hers.

Jemima felt as if the skies opened and there was the music of a celestial choir, while the light of the sun, the moon, and the stars all rolled into one to envelop her in a glory that was beyond words.

She felt as if the Viscount took possession of her and she was no longer herself but a part of him.

She knew that her whole being poured out the love she had always had for him so that she gave him her heart, her soul, and her mind, and she was his completely and absolutely as she had always wanted to be.

He kissed her until he carried her far above the world and they were in a very special Heaven that Jemima had always known existed but had thought never to find.

Then at last the Viscount raised his head.

"My darling, my sweet!" he said unsteadily. "How can I lose you?"

"Do . . . you really . . . love me? I never . . . thought you . . . would."

"I love you as I did not know it was possible to love anybody," the Viscount said, "but I was not aware of it until Freddy told me he had asked you to go away with him."

"F-Freddy . . . told you . . . that?"

"He told me, and I felt like murdering him! But it was then that I knew I would never give you up to any man, even if you wanted me to."

"I should . . . never want . . . you to," Jemima whispered. "I love you . . . I have always loved you . . . ever since the first moment I . . . saw you."

"I wish I were able to say the same thing," the Viscount said, "but I was such a fool that I went on imagining that I was in love with your cousin even after she had treated me like dirt!"

"But . . . she is . . . so beautiful!"

"Not half as lovely as you are!" the Viscount said firmly. "And I will tell you the one thing I love more than anything else about you, and which I missed unbearably while you have been away."

"What is . . . that?"

"Your laughter, my precious. I had grown so

used to hearing it, and to laughing with you, that suddenly when you were gone, everything was dull and silent and I was alone and lonely as I have never been in the whole of my life!"

Jemima pressed herself against him.

"Please . . . forgive me . . . and let me . . . come home."

"It is not a question of *letting* you," the Viscount replied. "I am *taking* you home. If you had refused to come I would have dragged you back, if there had been no other way—with a rope round your neck!"

Jemima laughed and the sound seemed to lilt through the small room.

"Oh, wonderful, wonderful Valient, it is the sort of thing that only you would say, and exactly what I would . . . want you to . . . say to me."

"I mean it!" the Viscount said firmly. "And let me make this quite clear, Jemima—if I find you flirting with Freddy I swear I will call him out! You are my wife and I do not intend to allow you to forget it!"

"As though I should!" Jemima cried. "I love you, Valient. I love you until now that I am with you again, the whole world is golden with sunshine and filled with happiness!"

"That is what I wanted you to say," the Viscount said. "But now for God's sake let us get home. People are pouring into the Spa and we have to keep sending to London for more cans and flagons, and there are a dozen invitations asking us to dine with people in the County. I am fed up with trying to cope with everything on my own!"

"You will not have to any more," Jemima said. "Oh, darling, darling Valient, is it really...true that I can come back to the Priory . . . and be with . . . you?"

"You are coming back!" the Viscount answered. "And I do not intend to waste any more time talking about it. Have you got a bonnet or something?"

He looked round the School-Room and Jemima gave a little gurgle of laughter.

"I shall have to go to the cottage where I am lodging to collect my things and to thank Mrs. Barnes for having me."

"Well, hurry up!"

"I suppose you have come here in Freddy's Phaeton?"

"What else did you expect?"

"You never...told me how you...found me."

"It was Emily who guessed where you had gone."

"Emily!" Jemima exclaimed.

"She came to see you because she is not happy with the Roseburgs and wants to work for you again. I promised that if I could find you where she thought you would be, we would employ her."

"I would love to have Emily, but can we... afford it?"

"If you could see the amount of money we are taking at the Spa! We will soon be able to afford not only Emily but a Cook and a Butler!"

"I do not believe you!"

"It is true! The Spa has caused a sensation, but I have not been able to enjoy thinking about it because I was wondering and worrying about you."

"I must come back at once!" Jemima said. "I suppose Emily remembered when I talked to her about my mother and father and how happy we had been at Lower Maidwell before I had to go and live with my uncle."

"That is exactly what she remembered," the Viscount said, "and I shall certainly keep my promise and take her into our employment."

Jemima smiled at him and he went on:

"There is another person I am going to employ for the rest of my life, and who will never be able to give in her notice."

Jemima gave a little laugh of sheer happiness. Then she said:

"I never ... never want to ... leave you again! Oh, Valient ... if you only knew how unhappy I have been without you ... and how frightened I was for the future."

"If you have suffered, then it is entirely your own fault!" the Viscount said.

He meant to sound severe but his voice was tender, and as if he could not help himself he put out his arms and drew Jemima once more close against him.

"I love you!" he said. "That is something I want to go on saying over and over again, every minute, every second of the day, until I make you sure of it. You are mine, Jemima, and I cannot live without you."

"That is what I wanted you to say ... but thought I would never ... hear it. Only, darling, I wish I were rich ... so that you could buy all the things you ... really want."

"I have everything I want—now," the Viscount

said, pulling her closer. "You may find this hard to believe, Jemima, but when I was driving here today, I was thinking that being poor with you is much more fun than if I were rich."

"Do you . . . really mean . . . that?"

"I really mean it! It has been an amusement I have never known before to make the Priory habitable again, to open the spring, and even to cart all that damned gravel which you made me do!"

He suddenly crushed her against him so that her breath was squeezed out of her body.

"Love me!" he ordered. "I want your love and I know now it is everything I want in the whole world."

"You know I . . . love you," Jemima answered against his lips.

She thought he would kiss her but he said:

"It has all been an amazing, exciting adventure, just as you told me it would be! Also there is so much more for us to do in the future, and everything will be marvellous because we are doing it together."

Then he bent his head and kissed her passionately, demandingly, and possessively.

She found there was a fire on his lips that had not been there before, and she felt the flicker of a little flame within herself respond to it.

It was so exciting, so thrilling, that she knew this was another side of the love which she had longed for and which too was part of God.

"I love . . . you . . . I love . . . you," she said first in her heart, then aloud as he released her lips.

"And I love you!" he replied. "For Heaven's

sake let us go home so that I can make love to you properly. We have wasted too much time as it is!"

He took his arms from her as he spoke, and, taking her hand, began to pull her towards the door.

"Come on!" he said. "Quickly!"

As he hurried her down the path so that she was running beside him, she could see the Phaeton waiting for them in the road.

"But . . . Valient . . ." she protested, "I must tell Mrs. . . ."

"We are going home!" the Viscount said firmly.

When they reached the Phaeton he picked her up in his arms and dumped her on the seat.

As he did so, he drew sixpence out of his pocket and threw it towards the boy who had been holding his horses, then climbed in and brought the whip down on them.

They jumped forward, and as the wheels began to roll, causing a great cloud of dust to billow out behind them, Jemima cried:

"My clothes! And I must tell the Vicar where I am going!"

"I am taking you home!"

He turned to have a quick look at her and added:

"Home—my adorable little wife, where you belong!"

As she laughed up at him because his behaviour was so ridiculous and at the same time so wonderful, he bent towards her and his lips held hers fiercely and possessively.

Then as they drove on, the Viscount was laughing.

About the Author

Barbara Cartland, the celebrated romantic novelist, historian, playwright, lecturer, political speaker, and television personality, has now written well over two hundred and eighty books as well as recently recording an album of love songs with the London Philharmonic Orchestra. In private life she is a Dame of Grace of St. John of Jerusalem, has fought for better conditions and salaries for mid-wives, has championed the cause of old people, and has founded the first Romany Gypsy Camp in the world. Barbara Cartland is deeply interested in Vitamin Therapy and is President of the British National Association for Health.